JACKSON

By Lynn McLaughlin

◆ FriesenPress

Suite 300 - 990 Fort St
Victoria, BC, V8V 3K2
Canada

www.friesenpress.com

ISBN
978-1-5255-7498-6 (Hardcover)
978-1-5255-7499-3 (Paperback)
978-1-5255-7500-6 (eBook)

1. FICTION, FAMILY LIFE

Distributed to the trade by The Ingram Book Company

"Having children just puts the whole world into perspective. Everything else just disappears."

Kate Winslet

ACKNOWLEDGMENTS

The fictional characters in this book evolved through conversations with many people; those fighting to be mentally well, parents of young adults experiencing mental illness, and breast cancer survivors. Getting to know each of them and walking through their experiences, fears, and triumphs has been heartbreaking and inspiring. Sincere appreciation is extended to fellow author, Yvonne Marrs. Many of the perspectives of *Jackson* were developed through her insights, experience, and passion.

From Yvonne MARRS

As an author and a chronic-illness sufferer, I have the experiences to help people suffering with depression and anxiety, and the ability to make it readable, relatable, and understandable. I really want to produce a book about my own life's experiences in order to help others, and so I was delighted to be able to help shape this tale, so that it will strike a chord with many readers. As with other illnesses, everyone feels differently; people have varying tolerances and thresholds—and therefore boundaries. You cannot second-guess mental health, and you should never try. Never judge someone until you have walked a mile in their shoes, as the saying goes.

Yvonne Marrs

INTRODUCTION

Wouldn't it be wonderful if all childhood maladies had the simple fix we all remember? Maybe some Tylenol to bring down a temperature or a little bit of cough syrup to ease a croupy cough. If things became more serious, a trip to the doctor or even the emergency room, where medical personnel could tell you both what was wrong and what you could do about it. Behind it all, was the parent's kiss to the forehead, ostensibly to check for a fever but we all knew it provided a wonderful sense of safety and security in the knowledge that our parents were there and would take care of whatever assailed us.

That would be wonderful but unfortunately, life is not always so simple, particularly when a parent and child are faced with navigating the confused, oftentimes terrifying world of mental health.

In the pages that follow Lynn McLaughlin brings decades of experience as a talented and highly respected educator, and perhaps most importantly a mother to the forefront, as she does a deep dive into the lives of June and Jackson. A mother and a son who find themselves wandering through the constantly evolving landscape of acute and chronic mental health.

While *Jackson* is certainly fictional it is no less an accurate portrayal of the unique and personal battle that is fought by every family member who has undertaken to understand, to help, and to love when faced with the unthinkable. At times painful and frustrating to read, *Jackson* is also a book filled with the characteristic compassion and humanity that McLaughlin herself has brought to every aspect of her own professional and personal life.

Perhaps most importantly this book not only provides a stark and realistic depiction of how mother and son are dealing with

Jackson's mental health, it also provides the reader with a vision of hope — a potential pathway through the systemic and very personal landmines inherent in Jackson and June's world — towards understanding and acceptance. McLaughlin puts a human face on the very fears, anxieties, and self-doubt that are ubiquitous in the world of mental health.

For those of you who have lived this experience, that face will be all too familiar. For those of you who have not, that face will aid you in developing a greater understanding of and compassion for those who demand your support.

For all of us *Jackson* is a stark but clear guide as to how one family found a way to adjust their world view to first acknowledge and then to ultimately accept the realities of mental health and through it all maintain a deep and abiding love for one another.

Rest assured, *Jackson* provides no simple fixes. There is no Tylenol or cough syrup and trips to the doctor or to the emergency room don't always provide much in the way of understanding for Jackson or June. But through it all, McLaughlin provides the reader with her own version of the kiss to the forehead. In its entirety, Jackson provides a sense of safety and security in the knowledge that there are pathways through the convoluted and terrifying world of mental health. While there may not be the simple fix of childhood, there are ways that can and do nurture compassion and love.

There is always hope.

Alan Goyette, MSW, RSW
Clinical Social Worker

This book is dedicated to YOU...
Whether you are desperate to save your child
or struggling to figure out who you are...
Talk openly about it.
Be empowered.
You are never alone.

TABLE OF CONTENTS

CHAPTER ONE

"Fear is a powerful beast but we can learn to ride it."

Justine Musk

Jackson

I was always angry as a kid. I can't describe it in any other way except to say that it was rough. I don't remember why I felt the way I did, only that I did everything I could to control myself so no one would laugh or make fun of me. It was worse in school; I didn't want to leave my desk some days. I didn't even go to the bathroom. At recess, I'd find a way to stay inside and do work or help in another class, so I didn't have to be out there and take a chance at getting picked on. What if someone made fun of me? Laughed at me in front of the whole school? Outside, there was no one close enough to stop kids if they wanted to pick on me.

One time, the teacher asked me a question, and I was pretty sure I was right. Why did she ask me? I didn't have my hand up. I always looked down when she asked questions. I hated talking in front of big groups of people. My answer was wrong. When we had to take turns reading out loud, I'd count the number of kids ahead of me so I could practice my part before my turn. Stupid. Idiot.

When I got home, I let loose. I didn't care who heard me or if I got sent to my room. I couldn't stand it anymore. None of the other kids were around, so I didn't have to hold it all in anymore. It all spilled out. I blew up again and again, calling my parents names. It made me feel better until the next day. And the next one. And the next one. I knew I was different. Never focussed. Always worried. No one else was like that, right?

June

As a family of three, our lives were thrown more than enough highs and lows. Craig and I met at a concert on my twenty-fifth birthday. This six-foot tall, slim man with an incredibly broad smile happened to have a seat beside me. Confident young people, entering our careers, and jumping at each opportunity, we married eighteen months later, madly in love. Craig began his own business as an electrician, and I was establishing myself as an investment counsellor. My new husband was kind in nature, driven, intelligent, and loved to get his hands dirty. He was never one to beat around the bush—telling things exactly as he saw them.

We settled on the outskirts of London, Ontario and were blessed with our son, Jackson. He was healthy, happy, and energetic, playing and learning from anything in his grasp. As he grew into a toddler, with an inquisitive personality emerging, we dreamt of his future; a leader, advocate, volunteer—the world would be his to change. He would be a confident, proud adult, firm in his beliefs, with the highest level of integrity.

As a young child, Jackson's temper tantrums were extreme. He pulled pictures off his walls and clothing out of his drawers, throwing everything around the bedroom. He screamed that he hated us and everyone else. Each time—exhausting. We fell into a routine where one of us took charge and the other stepped back, waiting him out, sometimes for a full hour. Craig and I questioned ourselves and each other as parents. What were we doing wrong? Why hadn't we seen these behaviours coming? What could we change or do differently? From laughing about something that had happened during our day, to an episode which too often ended with one of us blaming each other for triggering our son. We attributed Jackson's outbursts to him not getting his way, which is typical for youngsters. He would outgrow them, or so we thought.

Our son was extremely sensory driven as a child. The seams had to be cut out of every garment because they bothered him. In kindergarten, he would come home from school, take off his clothes, and walk around the house in his pyjama pants, holding a favourite stuffed ninja turtle. At bedtime, we had a set routine, which was posted up in his room; snack... bath...brush teeth... snuggle time to read... wall light left on...door propped open...treasured blanket and ninja in hand. Anything outside of that routine caused issues and Jackson would call out, unable to sleep.

As he grew older, his tantrums occurred much more frequently and almost always shortly after he arrived home from school. I was working from home, so bore the brunt of his volatility. It's expected as a natural part of child development, isn't it? But to what age?

At dinner one evening, out of nowhere, he began to yell, threw his fork across the room, knocked over his chair, and stormed down the hall, slamming the bedroom door. We were dumbfounded. We had no idea what might have caused such an extreme outburst when all we were doing was talking about an electrical job Craig was working on.

Staring at our food, we stayed at the table as he screamed from his room. For the first time we were both afraid. He could have hurt himself or someone else. Craig and I stared at each other in disbelief, visibly shaken. Craig wanted us to wait him out and I tried. I couldn't stand hearing our son yelling like that. When it sounded as though something fell off the wall, it was too much to bear.

Jackson was sitting on the floor beside his bed crying. I left the bedroom door open behind me but barely entered. He began to calm as I waited. He was sorry for throwing his fork, but would not, or could not, tell me what had caused him to blow up. He did not want to hurt anyone but was so angry. The turmoil he was facing emotionally was becoming detrimental to his well-being and ours. Craig and I both agreed that night that it was time to dig deeper.

We met with school staff who had been seeing no concerning behaviours. They noted nothing but a hard-working, caring child. He was fairly strong academically and had just become involved in track and field at school. Jackson had also been playing house-league hockey in our community. Socially, he had a few friends that stuck together. How could our child behave perfectly well at school and have such extreme eruptions at home?

Our first medical appointment with the family physician resulted in a referral to a pediatrician. Rating scales, check lists, and a full physical check-up were done. All new to us but we did what was rec-ommended. I began to consult with his teachers more often, by phone and in meetings right after school, documenting every outburst or concern. We wondered if there was something happening behind the scenes socially. Jackson disclosed that he did not use the bathrooms at school all day. He thought they were dirty. Explosive episodes esca-lated and we thought we were coping, until the day Jackson punched his fist through a wall in his bedroom as he screamed obscenities. Enough was enough.

At this point we requested to have a full psychological assessment, which was completed over several sessions with Jackson, Craig, and me. I had been keeping everything in a file and at first, I pulled out some of my notes. What would she think of us as parents? I ended up sharing everything with her, begrudgingly. The psychologist con-cluded that Jackson was an anxious child. Anxious? Wouldn't he have wanted to stay home, not go to school or play sports? We learned that anger is one of the ways that anxiety can manifest itself. Jackson was excessively worried and didn't have the skills to cope, which lead to frustration and anger. There was no formal diagnosis, but we were given recommendations to help him and the family deal with his fears. They included keeping him active in sports and maintaining regular appointments with a child therapist, who would teach him strategies and techniques. We would follow up as recommended, learning as well. Hoping that by knowing what to expect would lessen his worry, Jackson was given advance warning if our routine was changing in any way.

Although he was successful in school, the build-up of stress over the day was not healthy. It made sense to us. Jackson was excessively worried about things, to the point where he felt defeated. He held his emotions in all day, until he came home to where he felt safe and could release what had been building up for so many hours. While we were relieved to finally understand what was happening to our son, we wished we had sought help much sooner—Jackson had been suffering.

The child counsellor worked with Jackson over several months to help him understand his own emotions and learn to use strategies to de-escalate. Teachers were supportive in giving him breaks when needed, checking in on him more often to ensure he understood instructions and providing the positive feedback he needed.

At that time, Craig and I made a decision—one that I regret today. We chose not to share the formal written report with our son. He was twelve years old and we thought the medical jargon would be overwhelming. We did not want to focus on the label of "anxiety," but on what we could do to teach our son to be aware and proactive.

Were we protecting Jackson or was it our way of postponing acceptance? Did we think that the counselling and follow up would "fix" our son? It was a mistake. I wish we would have asked the psychologist to meet with all three of us. She could have helped Jackson understand her findings in language he would have understood at that time. If we used the term anxiety naturally as we did with any other illness, perhaps Craig and I could have worked with the child counsellor to help Jackson accept and learn to cope with this diagnosis from the beginning.

Jackson

I thought I was supposed to be learning to calm down. At the beginning, he kept asking me to play a stupid card game with him. It wasn't a regular game. I picked a card that told me to finish the start of the sentence or another one with a question. I had done a couple of paintings and he asked me how they made me feel or why I drew something the way I did. I just painted. It didn't mean anything. Seemed like a total waste of time.

After a few meetings, though, we started to play a game he called mindfulness. That was a new one for me. We pretended I was upset about something and I practiced taking time to think about what I needed to do and say then we talked about it.

When we were almost done our meetings, Mom or Dad came in to join us. It was kind of fun then. At school, I tried to remember what I was learning. It felt like it was helping a little bit.

June

Secondary school increased the complexities of Jackson's life. There were new rules to learn, new subjects, new ways of working through the day. The school building itself was almost new and it was large, easily confusing for incoming students. It created an anxious frame of mind in our only child. "I'll never find my way to class. I'll never get to the cafeteria in time to join the lunch line. I'll never remember my timetable or my locker number. I'll never find the gym." To cope with these anxieties, he visited the school several times with friends the week before school started. Feeling a combination of excitement and fear, he walked the halls and located the classrooms, his locker, and any other place of interest. We also suggested he meet with his resource teacher, who would be his go-to person when he needed help with his courses.

Socially, he had a core group of friends who were strong students, athletes, and well rounded. Jackson was successful in joining the hockey team and even in grade nine was on the ice for a lot of the game. He drew energy from his teammates and became one of the most recognized players in the school. He put incredible pressure on himself to be the best—to never be benched. In some ways he drew strength from his talent, but he endured a great deal of stress, never wanting to disappoint his team or coach. If he made a mistake, which was rare, it was written all over his face. Jackson was harder on himself than anyone else could ever have been.

Outside of hockey season, he became a very committed runner. I can't recall the number of times I suggested he go for a run when he was upset. It clearly calmed him, and I think, kept him somewhat grounded. Although I'm not a runner, walking in the fresh air on trails always helped me to reduce my own stress. Being in nature does make us feel better emotionally. No noise, nothing drawing us in. It's made a difference in my own daily outlook.

Jackson

Part of our training when I was on the track and field team was running as a warmup. I ate it up, not wanting to run with anyone else and keeping a quicker pace. I started running on my own, to stay in good shape and escape. I ran at least three times a week and got stronger and faster.

When I ran, I thought about my problems. They just seemed so much clearer to me. If I was in a bad mood or pissed off, I felt a lot better. If I had a headache, running got rid of it. I got pumped up us I reached each goal. My parents would tell me to go for a run if I was angry or grumpy. They were right, I came back feeling happier and less tense. Springbank Park became my favourite running route. I usually stayed on the path, but sometimes took off, running through the nearby forest. The river flowing… trees hiding me from everyone … wild animals scampering to find food… quiet sounds all around me. It was calming and cleared my head. I never felt out of control when I was running.

June

Jackson was permitted to go to a small room to write all his tests at school, which alleviated some of his academic worries. He did not hesitate to do so, and often met with teachers to get extra help. When oral presentations were required, he gave them after class with only the teacher present, or he handed them in electronically. Blow-ups still happened, but the frequency diminished. By then we understood they were linked to his stressors. We no longer considered them "behavioural."

CHAPTER TWO

"Tell a lie once, and all your truths
become questionable."

Author Unknown

"The ultrasound and mammogram results confirm that you have breast cancer." Those words will be forever ingrained in my memory—a moment when time stood still.

Craig and I had been called in for a medical consultation. We weren't naïve, about it. We were frightened but prepared for the worse. We foolishly believed having this mindset would mean that anything we were told would be easier to handle.

At home the previous Monday, I didn't have any clients scheduled and I was sketching in the backyard, a hobby of mine. It was a peaceful morning with the sun cascading through the trees, but I had this odd sense that something wasn't right. As I showered shortly thereafter, I found several lumps in my right breast.

I did not hesitate to call the doctor and was seen that afternoon. My doctor immediately sent me for an ultrasound. After that, he ordered a mammogram before I even left the office. As I watched him write up the order I froze and stopped breathing. I began to tremble and lost all colour in my face.

There was no question that something was definitely wrong, and I was spinning with all the possibilities.

Craig was with me and he squeezed my hand as the doctor talked to us. It's all a blur to me. My husband held me as I broke down, sobbing in the office for quite some time, reeling in disbelief.

The doctor left us alone for a while and when he returned, we had countless questions to ask. Cause? Options? Second opinion? Long term? Prognosis? He answered every question to the best of his ability, giving us the time we needed, but he was not a cancer specialist. There would be a referral to an oncologist, along with a CT and bone scan. We needed to know if this cancer had metastasized. Not only did I have the BIG C, but there was a chance it had already spread to other areas of my body.

What do you do with that news? The possibility of death terrified me. What would my son do without a mother? We all know we are going to die someday, but I had never actually thought about it. I was too young and wouldn't even need to contemplate it for at least a decade. Or so I thought.

Jackson was fifteen years old and genuinely affected by the series of events and confusion thrown into our lives. Naturally, he was frightened of losing his mother. We consulted on how to share information and what we should tell him as surgery and treatments took over. Jackson had been doing quite well for some time. We were so afraid this would cause a relapse.

Jackson handled the news like a champion, in front of us anyway. Regardless of his bravado, though, we knew he would need support. We arranged for him to see a social worker regularly, which I believe helped tremendously. One of his teachers, also his hockey coach, became another set of ears and eyes for us.

Jackson was close with one of his cousins, Todd, who lived only a few blocks away. During my illness, Todd hung out with him, walking him home from school and often staying for the evening. He was a true friend in every sense of the word, and I really don't know what might have happened if he had not been there for Jackson

The advice given to us was to respond to Jackson's questions when they were asked, which would be an indication that he wanted the answers. We did everything possible to maintain his daily routines, a valiant attempt to shelter him from our new reality.

The oncologist advised me to have an immediate mastectomy followed by chemotherapy and radiation. After copious amounts of research, I insisted on an alternative plan and chose to endure six months of chemotherapy as a first step. I learned how to give myself daily injections to keep my white blood-cell count high enough. The injections took from my own bones, causing constant pain. Anti-nausea pills and steroids … a weekly cycle of hell. When my hair began to fall out, I felt alone, helpless. No one in my family could possibly understand. Not even my sister. They weren't living it. Only I was.

I was mentally and physically spent, but I couldn't let my family and friends see how I really felt. In public, I put on a brave face, giving short, non-committal answers to people who asked how I was doing. My brain was already in overdrive because of the fight. Everyone knows that cancer is a battle of life and death. People were kind and forgiving of my mood swings, cancellations of visits or calls, or tumbling emotions. Craig continued to work, but he was always by my side when I needed him. I had to refer my investment clients to someone else, which meant no income as I was self-employed.

I had to find a way to deal with the cascade of emotions I was feeling. I often sat up at night, out on the deck wrapped in a blanket. What would the next day bring? How could I find the strength I needed? There were periods of time when I was so ill, I stayed at my sister's home to protect my son. He didn't need to witness my suffering.

Mom went to my aunt's house for a few days of rest. What did that mean? Why did she send me a text message and not tell me herself? Why did she go without saying goodbye? Did this mean she wasn't coming back? Was she much worse than she wanted us all to believe? I felt I needed to do more to help Mom. She was in pain and I couldn't stand seeing her like that. She didn't deserve it. She was a good person. What could I do, though? It's not like I didn't try. I did everything she asked me to do, and I kept quiet while she slept and brought her coffee in her favourite mug.

Then I thought, wait a minute. Maybe if I did more, she wouldn't need to leave. Had she left because of me? But what? What did she need? What could I do? It was so unfair. Why couldn't they just fix her?

I mean, the doctor gave her the pills to work. It was Mom's idea to not have the surgery right away. I kind of thought that was a good thing—who wants to be in a hospital? They're scary places full of pained, suffering groans and the smell of death. It made me sick just thinking about it.

Even the doctor's office was a scary place when you saw people come out of there sobbing, crying, breathless, and gasping in fear. That's how I thought Mom would have been when they told her. Maybe Dad too, but I wasn't sure. Of course, he'd be upset, everyone would be upset, even the toughest person in the world.

Obviously, Mom and Dad put on their brave faces and skirted the issue, so as not to worry me. But how could I not worry? They were worried sick themselves; I could tell from Mom's stance. They gave me vague information, never fully answering my questions. Was Mom going to die? I needed to know.

Even after the pills and the surgery, there was still a chance, right? Maybe nobody could answer that question. Maybe they had many unanswered questions of their own, so I shouldn't ask anymore. I looked it up online and of course the statistics said that treatment was improving all the time, but was Mom in a high-risk group, or not? When she started losing her hair, I couldn't look at her at first. Her face stood out, so pale and thin.

Would Dad be able to cope without Mom? That was a scary thought—being left with only Dad. I mean, he was competent, owning his own business and everything, but he couldn't even run the vacuum cleaner. How would he help me with homework? Would he be able to pick me up from practices or take me to the games? Could he be a single parent and run his business and the house? Mom said that was a full-time job, plus he needed to be here for me.

Sacrifices would have to be made. Would it mean that I had to stop things, like hockey? I could still run, but I liked being part of a team…It wasn't fair that the things I loved to do might have to end.

Oh my God, what about the tuition I would need? Without that, I'd be a failure. I wouldn't be able do anything.

Would we have money problems without Mom? Many people struggle with money, especially single parents. You heard a lot of stories about them.

And then, who would support me? Dad couldn't. Dad got the guy stuff, but I didn't think he really got what I needed to calm down and not blow up or lose it.

Would Aunt Denise step in? Could she? Or…would we become one of those families who everyone feels sorry for and goes out of their way to help? How embarrassing would that be! That couldn't happen. Would Dad have to give up his business or get another job? One where he could earn lots more and work enough to still be home?

And then what about him? Could he cope alone? Probably not, he'd have to find another woman. There are masses of horror stories about bad stepmoms. Oh my God, I couldn't even begin to think about that…

I couldn't breathe. My heart hurt. Was this what a heart attack felt like? I was too young. What was happening? No one was home and I was shaking, curled up on the floor. I stared at the poster of Steve Yzerman on the wall above my head. I was going to pass out. Where was my phone? I couldn't move. I was so hot.

Focus.

I stared at Steve and tried to take deep breaths. One…two… three…four. It got less foggy…I was getting better.

Time to sit back up. What the hell was that? I couldn't tell them about it. There was too much already going on. I had to sleep. I'd wake up when someone got home.

I got knocked down time and time again, but I got back up; beaten, exhausted, but driven. Sometimes it me took longer to land on my feet or find that positive mindset, but I faced that monster. Chemotherapy, a mastectomy, and radiation treatments were successful. I not only beat that cancer, I killed it and as of this writing I have been well for over ten years. I will never be the same person I was before that disease. Worrying about losing my life gave me a whole new perspective. Anything that I previously considered a bother doesn't even matter anymore. I am grateful every day for the life that was given back to me, and for so many things that I took for granted. But I truly believe my cancer was one of the underlying factors contributing to Jackson's mental illness[1]. When I was well enough to work again, I sent a letter to each of my clients. A colleague had taken over their portfolios during my absence. Thankfully, the majority returned to me without question, almost in celebration. Each time I received another call, it drove me forward. Our lives returned to our new normal, but with increased concerns over our son's well-being.

Jackson had begun to experience panic attacks. I went to check on him one afternoon and he didn't answer when I knocked. "You're running late, bud," I said as I knocked, opening his door. He was just getting up off the floor, drenched in sweat, pale and shaken. What was happening? He sat up on the bed and confessed it wasn't the first time. How could he have kept this from us? He said that he was freezing up, trembling, and sweating, all while struggling to breathe. How could we not have known? These extreme physical symptoms happen when someone is faced with a frightening situation, perhaps something they experienced in the past that caused anxiety or fear. We knew what some of those triggers were. My illness? The fear of losing his mother? Visits to the hospital? School? Whatever they were, they were crippling our son.

It started with a couple of guys at the arena that I recognized from school. I was just hanging out watching a game of hockey. They offered me a joint. Why not? I was young but didn't give a damn. It was legal for me a couple of years later so what could it hurt? What would the cops do, give me a warning? We were around back where no one would see us. I coughed at first. They laughed and I almost took off. But then it hit me. Another toke. A third. My muscles relaxed and I laughed, chuckled almost. They say smoking weed feels different for everyone. There's no way I would have a panic attack feeling like this – relaxed and happy! I was lying on the clouds with nothing to even think about.

CHAPTER THREE

"We all wear masks, and the time comes when we cannot remove them without removing some of our own skin."

André Berthiaume

Jackson grew into a strikingly attractive young man, with long, dirty-blond hair and captivating blue eyes. It was his grade-twelve year with all the difficult decisions that come with it—what to do in post-secondary. He grappled with what field to enter, which school to attend. Should he live at home and choose a local college or university? Could he move away, live on campus, and cope with the anxiety such a move would bring? Regardless of his choice, we knew he would still need to have help to succeed in school. We broached the subject of another formal assessment and gave him some time to think about it.

Another full psychological/educational assessment was done over three sessions—three sessions that he had to build himself up to. In his mind, he had to excel. They had to see what he was capable of. Before each session he was terrified that he would have a panic attack.

He had some tools to build his strength and resilience and he used them. Running always helped. With the help of the psychologist, we ensured that he knew what was going to happen at each appointment. He was most relieved to know that only one person would be working with him and he could take a break at anytime. He could even end the session if he needed to. Having options gave him control.

The psychologist gathered information from us, his teachers, and, of course, Jackson. This time, Jackson was formally diagnosed with Anxiety Disorder[2]. The recommendations that the psychologist brought forward would be helpful to him, *if he implemented them.* There were detailed academic accommodations Jackson would be entitled to should he attend a post-secondary school. He would be able to write all exams in a quiet location, could request an extension of deadlines, would not be expected to present in front of large groups, and would have someone in the student services office as a key contact should there be issues.

I can't believe my parents kept this a secret for so long. I thought it was all me. I couldn't control my own emotions and blamed myself because I blew up all the time. I couldn't figure out why or what to do to stop it from happening. I tried. Running helped, but I could have done so much more if I'd known. All along I had anxiety. Why didn't they tell me? I get that I was still in elementary school, but still. Why didn't that counsellor tell me when I saw him all the time? Things could have been so much different and better. How could they have done this to me? It was my brain, not me! It was their fault I was the way I was. Wasn't it that doctor's job to tell me the truth? Did they have any idea what it was like to not be able to breathe? To almost pass out in front of everyone? To drench your shirt in sweat? I wouldn't have been having these attacks if I'd known it was my brain all along. I wouldn't want to smoke weed to stop them from coming. It's not me. I'm not crazy.

I couldn't trust anyone anymore.

Still living at home, Jackson adjusted well in the first year. He ran regularly, played pick-up sports at the gym, and seemed genuinely happy. He achieved all course credits and carried an average of just over seventy percent. Many of his friends had moved away and he went out less frequently, but we weren't concerned. The work he needed to do for school was quite time-consuming.

To us, he was finding a new way of balancing demands.

Year two of college…confident, finding success, using the accommodations he needed, Jackson decided to move into an apartment with two roommates on the opposite side of the city of London. He was certain this was his next step. We were concerned but supported him. It was a huge decision for someone who had struggled, but he was as ready as he would ever be and working towards his Environmental Diploma.

Chris, one of his friends, had moved into an apartment the year before, and when a room became available, he invited

Jackson to join him and another roommate. Chris was somewhat aware of Jackson's mental illness; the challenges and triumphs, but to what degree I'm not certain. I saw my son wearing a mask at that time. He appeared strong and brave. Moving out of the family home had to be an enormous stressor for someone with anxiety. He would not want to blow up in front of his roommates. What would he do to release that tension?

Chris and I had been buddies for years. He and my cousin Todd were the two who understood me; and the ones I talked to the most. Mom knew this, which is why she was happy I was moving in with someone we knew, not just two strangers. She didn't know that Chris and I had smoked together.

Carl, the other roommate, was someone I didn't know until I moved in. But in fact, Carl was chill. He and Chris both helped me move in some stuff, and then we ordered pizza and had a drink in the kitchen. I tried to think that Carl wouldn't judge me until he got to know me himself. Always overthinking.

It wasn't as scary as I thought it would be, I must admit. I knew the area. I knew Chris and was getting to know Carl; the people who would be around me the most. I was in the swing of college and I'd made friends from the course and the pickup hockey games that I was starting to play.

Chris knew of my struggles. I was sure he would help if I needed him, although I wanted to believe that I could deal with things and not lose my self-control. At least I didn't want to think I couldn't cope...I mean, I could smoke if I wanted to. I wasn't alone. I had friends I trusted, and I had my parents to a degree, at the end of the phone, and either of them could be here after a short drive. I could also get home in a taxicab. But I wouldn't need to.

So yeah, this was what it was like to take an adult step. I'd left home, I was coming to grips with the college workload, and building my own future. Finally!

I was meeting new challenges. Most of my friends from high school had girlfriends by now, and some had moved into apprenticeships or full-time jobs which was pretty wild.

I'd dated on and off, but I never felt comfortable. My nerves always took over and I felt like an idiot all the time. What to say. How to act. It was easier not to date at all. Dad said there was plenty of time and that my focus had to be college. As if I could forget. What did he mean by that? He was just trying to ground me, and I needed that to step out on my own. Yeah, I had people to help me, but I needed to start doing stuff for myself. Other people could, so I could too. Right?

If I needed extra help, I could talk with the person at the college supporting me. I had my running, and I could focus on exercise as it had worked for me so often. I knew shit would come, and I would deal with it. I could smoke, but I didn't need to. I kept telling myself that.

I would be fine.

Jackson began that second year of college by competing in a marathon he had been training for, and he was thrilled with his success. We were so proud. It was a great example of what he could do with the right mindset, determination, and goals.

Knowing he had to be active to be well mentally and physically, he continued to run regularly, and he played pick-up hockey two evenings a week. He was proving to himself that he was good enough, that he would get somewhere in life. As he progressed through college, he would start a co-op placement in the community, but not until most of his formal courses were done. As the content of his academic studies became more challenging, Jackson started to question his abilities and flounder. Anxiety took over—ten-fold.

I was going to flunk out. Damn exams. I knew my stuff. Even when my head was on right and I was going to classes, I blew the exams. I made my own notes, breaking it all down so I could remember. Sometimes, I even came up with stupid sayings, to help.

I knew the night before an exam what was going to happen. I wouldn't get any sleep. If I went for a run, it was better, for a while…I couldn't smoke or I wouldn't even have shown up to write it. When I left for the exam. I talked to myself the whole way. "It's no big deal. You know it! So, what if you fail? Just do your best." It wasn't good enough. I couldn't do my best because I knew I could freeze up or end up crippled, struggling to breathe, hiding in the bathroom. Then I would have to find a way to get myself back together and just show up. If I didn't show up, I got ZERO! Zero, because of my anxiety. I knew I got to write in a place that was quieter. Not in a big room or gym. Fine. I told myself that's all I would need, but I was lying. That was bullshit. It was in my head. It was all in my head. Stop!

So, bottom line was that everyone else in my program was blowing the exams away. I knew I couldn't. I'd be lucky if I passed.

The only things that kept me going were the assignments. I could take my time, do them when I wanted to, and I almost always got a great mark. That was how I was passing. There had to be another way. I loved this program and I couldn't wait to work in the field. I couldn't really prove that to them, though. Not the way they had this system set up. Exams were worth like thirty percent sometimes. Why couldn't the assignments be worth that? I went to my case manager and she said I had all the accommodations I could get.

I learned to become friendly with the instructors. Even though they might never see my face, I always sent an email at the beginning of the semester to share my accommodations and thank them for being so understanding. Bottom line, I was at a disadvantage because of something I couldn't control. Something I couldn't do anything about. Should I have gone to the clinic every time and gotten a doctor's note because I was on the verge? What would that solve? It would just put off the inevitable. Why not let me start my co-op placement early, and I could show them what I could do when I wasn't stuck behind a desk? Half of the shit they were teaching us didn't matter anyway. I wouldn't ever use it. It was a waste of my time.

He made it to spring OK, and then began hanging out with some new friends he'd met at school. Young men and women who loved to get together and party—wherever and whenever. If we went back in time to when Craig and I were that age, that's exactly what each of us would have been doing. We were thrilled that he'd met new people and was having some fun for a change. He seemed so carefree and normal. After all his struggles with academics, why should we worry? He had been well for so long, winning in many ways by overcoming his fears and anxieties. Was he wearing a brave face as I had when I was ill, trying to keep everyone from knowing the truth?

CHAPTER FOUR

"Not everything that is faced can be changed. But nothing can be changed until it is faced."

James Baldwin

Jackson's mental health was quickly deteriorating, but we didn't know it. In our weekly conversations, he masterfully kept everything from us, pretending that he was fine. He knew when we would call, typically a Sunday night, and was sure to be sober. We were oblivious to the fact that he was regularly drinking to the point of passing out. Weren't there clues? Why did we not sense things were off? If one of us had dropped in for a visit now and then, we likely would have seen the reality of what he was doing to himself. Would we have sensed the fake smile he was painting on, noticed the smell of his breath?

How naïve we were. Jackson had begun binge drinking and was experiencing suicidal ideations. What had triggered this? Was it a series of small things that he just held on to, dwelling on them? Had feelings and demons from his past crept up that he could not deal with? Was he just trying to fit in and roll with the new crowd, or did the booze numb the anxiety, giving a false sense of calmness for a short period of time? Why hadn't Chris called us about it, or was Chris even aware? Was our son going to classes, or running at all?

Why was I so blind? Chris tried to tell me that I was spiraling, that my new friends were trash. He wanted nothing to do with them. At first, I stood up for them and defended myself. I like to party—so what? When I went out with them, I always needed to drink—so what? I never needed a drink when I was home. That was OK wasn't it? If you don't drink all the time, you're not an alcoholic.

My new friends and I had so many great nights. I don't remember a few—we were obliterated. That did bother me; that I didn't know where I was or what I did—but big deal. I felt free when I was drunk. I never worried about feeling nervous or anxious. When I drank one after another, it didn't matter how many people I was with. No tension. No worries. We laughed and did crazy stupid things. One night, I fell onto the road as a car was approaching. I do remember that because I was scared shitless for a second. Then I didn't give a damn. I got back up laughing and leading the way for another drink.

Until one morning when I woke up freezing on a park bench. No idea where I'd been. I'd passed out sometime in the night. They'd either left me there or I had wandered away. It didn't matter. I was covered in vomit, trembling as people walked by, staring. I was weak. I pulled the hood of my sweatshirt over my head as I ran behind a tree to throw up some more.

"Are you alright?" I heard from behind me.

I said nothing to the older man who had checked on me, and I walked as quickly as I could towards our apartment, searching my pockets for the keys. Thank God my roommates were not there when I got home. I stood in the shower and punched the wall, kicking myself for being so dumb. Did my friends know? I couldn't face them if they did. How could they have left me there like that? I tried to hide the evidence, washing my clothes, and cleaning the washroom before I crashed for hours.

Staying in my room let me avoid contact with people—total isolation. I had been lucky to wake up the way I did. Even my wallet was still in my pocket.

Then, a new brainstorm. Why not just drink at home? Safe. No one to worry about or judge me. I could crash when I wanted to, and it would feel good—for a little while anyway. Drinking in the middle of the day was for losers, right? But if I had a Coke and added a bit of vodka to give it a kick, who'd know? I'd get a boost from the caffeine and chill from the booze. Middle ground! "Think I'll have another. Well, a third won't matter. It's just for today. Just this once".

CHAPTER FIVE

"Worry never robs tomorrow of its sorrow, it only saps today of its joy."

Leo F. Buscaglia

That first time I called Mom to say I couldn't do this anymore; I don't ever remember feeling so totally lost. Nothing—hockey and my friends, running, Chris, Todd—nothing mattered anymore. I was numb to everything. Numb to life, like a hamster on a wheel going around and around in circles but going nowhere. I couldn't face doing that for the rest of my life. What would I do?

School. Homework. Friends. Crowds. Exams. Teachers. Doctors. Mom and Dad. I needed help all the time. Was I that hopeless? Could I not take care of myself?

The more I thought about it, the more I doubted myself. Were the guys letting me play hockey because they felt sorry for me? Were the instructors forced to give me extensions on homework? Why couldn't I have a girlfriend like everyone else? I kept drinking, one after the other. Why not?

Then Chris confronted me. He poured all the vodka down the drain and I didn't even argue with him. I knew he was right. I was missing classes, tests—a mess. I had to get my shit back in order, but I didn't know how. I honestly didn't even care…or maybe I did, just a little bit.

Mom would know what to do. She always did. I started to cry when I heard her voice and I couldn't speak. Pathetic, weak, idiot. There seemed only one escape. I wanted to die.

Chris stayed with me until my parents arrived. I wasn't sure if I wanted him to, but he gave me no choice.

The first call was one that will be forever ingrained in my heart and my memory. It was quite late, and I was turning off the lights, getting ready for bed. The phone rang, which set off my radar. We rarely received calls after ten p.m.

Jackson was mumbling, attempting to say something in between sobs. Alarmed, I initially thought he had been in an accident of some sort. I kept affirming, "I'm here," in as soft and quiet a voice as I could. It was all I could do to not start crying, but knew I had to be there for him. I thought that maybe if I modelled deep breathing, I could help him calm himself.

I manoeuvred over to the living room, where Craig had been reading. I didn't need to explain. My facial expression, nonverbal language, and words were telling. He knew Jackson was in crisis.

After some time, Jackson was still breathing heavily but able to speak. He was hard to understand, and I was sure he was drunk. He said he "couldn't do it anymore." He didn't want to live. He had had enough.

We knew we needed to keep him on the phone. I was in shock, but somehow kept going. Where had this come from? We were being taken back in time, but this time it was in a much more terrifying way. Our son wanted to take his own life.

Craig and I jumped into the car and drove to his apartment as I tried to keep him engaged in any conversation. We were reacting, moving on instinct. Craig had been desperately dialing his phone, trying to contact one of Jackson's roommates to no avail.

The streetlights flashed past us as we raced to our son, arriving in just over fifteen minutes. Doors slamming, we both bolted to the apartment entrance. I still had the phone against my ear as we knocked furiously on the door. It slowly cracked open as the security chain was unbolted and Jackson haltingly opened the door. Chris was standing in the doorway of his bedroom, and slowly closed it behind him as he went inside.

Jackson stood there for what seemed forever but was merely a second, avoiding eye contact, and looking down at the floor. He quickly turned, moving through the main living area to his room.

I walked into our son's darkened room first, with Craig behind me. Through dim lamp-light, our son appeared, turning towards us as he sat on the edge of the bed, dishevelled. Clothing was all over the floor of the darkened room and the air was thick and stale. Empty pop cans and vodka bottles were strewn everywhere.

Our son was much calmer now as I sat beside him, putting my arm over his shoulder. Craig stood before us, unsure of what to do. With a shaky voice, Jackson disclosed that he did not want to live anymore. "I can't deal with anything…I'm so tired…I just don't care." He told us he'd had a plan to take his life by overdose but stopped because he couldn't bear the thought of anyone finding him—knowing how traumatic it would be for Chris or Carl. He was crying for help.

We did not ask what happened. It didn't matter in that moment. I couldn't breathe, I was shaking. Craig's face was ashen with concern. Holding back our own tears, we both hugged Jackson as he stared down at the floor. No judgment, no questions, or rushing to act.

After a few minutes, Craig suggested he come with us to the hospital, and he immediately stood up and asked for a couple of minutes to get changed and gather some things. Craig stood at the bedroom door while he did so, not able to take his eyes off his son, still fearful he would do something rash.

It then seemed somber…oddly peaceful as we drove through the city. I sat in the back seat, holding Jackson's hand, repeating, "We're here for you…You are not alone…We're not going anywhere…We love you…You'll get through this."

As he stared out the window, slumped in the seat, Jackson showed no emotion and remained silent. If I could only read his mind. What would this night bring?

We entered the emergency room. As I held his hand, he began to trail behind me. The waiting area was full of visibly ill people, who all seemed to be staring at us as we approached the triage window. *Really?* I thought. *You want us to sit here in front of all these people and disclose verbally that our son wants to take his life?*

Jackson sat in the chair in front of the nurse. Craig and I positioned ourselves to block the view of many of the bystanders. Jackson spoke with a quiet voice in response to the questions asked. Our initial impression was wrong. The staff were wonderfully kind and immediately escorted us to a room where we would wait to see the physician on duty. We were relieved to have some space to ourselves but had no idea what to expect.

Time passed. Awkward silence. When the doctor arrived, we were asked to leave the room so Jackson could speak with the doctor privately. Jackson hesitated. Patiently and with compassion, the doctor shared that Jackson could have one or both of us back with him at any time if he wanted. He nodded with that reassurance.

We slowly stepped back, leaving the room, ensuring he knew we would be right around the corner. But I wanted to stay there, dammit! He needed us. The rational side of me knew that this protocol was in place for a reason. Would a teenager having suicidal thoughts disclose everything to a doctor if a parent were present?

Soon we were invited back into the room and told they were giving our son something to calm him and a temporary bed for the night. A psychiatrist would do a full assessment. We knew it would likely not happen until morning.

Jackson fell asleep while Craig and I paced, argued, and questioned ourselves and each other until after dawn. Why hadn't we seen this coming? What signs had we missed? Why hadn't we been checking on him in person? Our guilt would continue to torture us as we waited for answers.

While we had no idea what had been disclosed during the meeting between Jackson and the psychiatrist, Jackson was released to us before noon after assuring the practitioner that he was OK. His explanation was that he had had a panic attack and started drinking.

This did not add up. He had clearly been in bed for days maybe, drinking alone. For whatever reason, he was not telling us the truth and was minimizing the gravity of his actions. But whatever the triggers were, he had responded with a threat of suicide. Thank God he called me. He was not coping.

This was more than real. It was terrifying. I couldn't think clearly. We now had a "Safety Plan" as a family. Not a plan to escape a fire in our home. A plan to help keep our son alive. A plan that had no guarantees and that our son had full control of. Jackson needed to know what to do when he was feeling overwhelmed, other than binge drinking. If he could identify triggers and see the warning signs, he could use strategies to get support and follow his plan if he was in crisis.

Medication was introduced by the psychiatrist to help deal with the symptoms of depression[3]. Jackson, however, described himself as just not caring. Our hearts were breaking. "I just don't care, Mom. Don't you get it? It doesn't matter. Nothing matters." Imagine your child; one you have such hope and love for—not finding his place in the world. We needed to learn to listen without judgment and to validate how our son was feeling. This was the first of more incidents to come. We were the most important part of his support network. The plan worked. We had two more visits to the hospital emergency room. Not eating, binge drinking, having suicidal thoughts, or missing classes were clear signs that he needed intervention.

CHAPTER SIX

At any given moment you have the power to say, "This is not how my story will end."

Christine Mason Miller

I thought: I'm an adult; I cannot run away…I'm an adult; I cannot run away…I'm an adult; I cannot run away…But I really want to. But you can't. You have nowhere to go, with no money. You are no use to anyone, and nobody likes you. Except those who are using you until they've got enough from you to suit them. The truth hurts. Like a knife in the heart…The truth slapping you in the face. Hmm… Time to run.

Chris saw me lacing up my running shoes and asked me with a frown what I was doing—didn't I know it was almost ten-thirty p.m.? I nodded and said that I knew, I wouldn't be long. I just needed to get out and run so I could think. He didn't challenge me. He knew that I ran to get my mind clear.

When I got back, I could tell that the demons had been talking over the voices of reason, and I could differentiate now. I didn't need to drink. I told the bad things to f*ck off and began to pack my bag for the next day. Then I took a quick shower, fell into bed, and fell fast asleep.

Next morning, Chris checked on how I was and we went out after breakfast. It was great to hear someone genuinely say, "Have a good day" and "See you later." I guess what they say about the small things in life being the most important is right!

You question what you did wrong—what you could have done differently. You ask yourself repeatedly what you can do to save him. But you can't. It's out of your hands. We all need a purpose in life; a sense of fulfilment, a joy, a reason to get up in the morning, a reason to try. You can be so wrapped up in not feeling any of these things that you forget who you are and what you want to do. Had Jackson forgotten about the joy and happiness that his life had brought himself and others?

Jackson became our focus, our reason for being. Worry became the norm. For my own peace of mind I needed to speak with him daily to gauge his emotional state and make sure he was sober. I learned to pick up on the clues. Craig was adamant that I needed to give our son the space to figure things out for himself and wanted to believe that Jackson would contact us when he was in crisis, as we'd agreed to in his safety plan. But calling him was the only thing that gave me some sanity as we shouldered his burdens.

I was always uneasy, almost distressed. Was my phone battery getting too low? Did I have service? When I didn't have clients, I paced, glancing repeatedly at my phone. Was he OK? What was he doing? Who was he with?

I tossed and turned all through the night, often getting up to make sure we hadn't missed a call. On the other hand, never able to predict what was about to happen, I became short of breath every time his number lit up. It got to the point where I would drive across town to go by his apartment. I knew his course schedule and when he was supposed to be gone. Even when I thought he would be home; I'd scrutinize what I saw. Why were the curtains closed? If I'd had x-ray vision, life would have been so much easier. Or would it have?

Hoping to convince me not to drive by, Craig hid my car keys one night. My husband was the voice of reason, but despite his efforts to keep me calm, I could not get past the horror of what might happen. Another disagreement. Another fight between us.

I was desperate to connect the dots...wondering what we'd missed and what we could have done to change this path he was on. We couldn't see the pattern that had unfolded over time. First, a difficult birth, then hospital visits related to breathing issues, which began when he was four months old. A diagnosis of asthma, along with sensory issues and over-the-top emotional outbreaks. Then there'd been the assessment that confirmed some anxiety, with specific recommendations that we followed. And then, my breast cancer.

Was Jackson's mental illness a result of his inability to manage each of these stressors in his life? I liken it to a piece of glass. It is strong but also fragile. As more and more things are stacked upon it—it weakens and eventually breaks into pieces. The truth is, we will never know. We cannot go back and change things. We must learn to let go of what we cannot control.

We were only privy to what he told us or what we learned through others. The calls he made when in crisis happened in the middle of the night. He never sounded impaired. If I'd had an inkling that he had been drinking, we would have jumped in the car and headed for his place without question. But how many times could we do that? How would he learn to work through his feelings himself if we always ran to save him?

I learned how to help him calm himself. Ironically, it was by diverting the subject away from how he was feeling and talking about something that happened at home or in the community. At least two of these calls occurred the night before an exam. They were almost predictable. He was so afraid of failing. Not because he didn't know the answers, but because he thought he would not remember them. He'd be too worked up or he'd have a panic attack. "Let's talk this through," I would say after discussing trivial things to calm him. Step by step we would go over what he needed to do. Did he have time for a run in the morning? Could he walk to the exam location and get some fresh air? Could he arrive a few minutes early to prepare, take some deep breaths, and focus? Would listening to his favourite music help? Perhaps breakfast with Chris or Carl? A comedy podcast?

I would stay on the phone with him until he was OK. He would almost always settle, but his safe plan was clear. We would drive over to his place and consider a hospital visit if need be.

College became a cycle of non-attendance followed by his struggles to catch up. I was so proud of him for doing everything that he could to not only pass his courses but strive for the best possible mark—all while in emotional turmoil. His health was more important to us than the diploma, but regardless of how many times we suggested he take a semester off or move home, he would have no part of it.

Jackson met with his case manager at the college regularly and had extensions to most assignments and longer time to write tests. He fought to stay in school by using the tools at his disposal. Although his grades did slip, he was never faced with academic probation.

It took a year longer than expected for Jackson to complete the three-year program at the local college. A lower course-load each semester and summer classes meant he would be more likely to succeed. When he started his co-op placement, the pressures seemed to subside. In that last college year, he finally began seeing a counsellor and his mental health improved. He started running regularly again, easily finishing ten kilometers. He loved exploring in nature and socializing with his roommates and insisted on staying at the apartment until he graduated that April.

The convocation ceremony was a celebration of countless accomplishments. When Jackson's name was about to be called for him to accept his diploma, Craig was already kneeling in front of the stage, camera in hand. Freeze frame—a moment where everything was perfect. Our son, the graduate!

The party at our home afterward was full of laughter with Craig at the BBQ and me playing hostess. Jackson was carefree and visibly happy. He had risen above all of it!

It was done. I'd done it. I couldn't give up. If I had, I'd have nothing. What would college credits get you without a diploma? They would mean nothing, and I have no idea where I would have ended up. Living back at home? Hiding in my room? I didn't have to think about that now. I'd never have to sit through an exam again. I'd never have to talk in front of a huge group of people or fight with a teacher for what I should have gotten without having to even ask for it. I felt better than being high or getting drunk, like nothing could pull me down. I didn't care that it took me a year longer than it should have. I'd get a job in no time. Couldn't wait. It was time to make some money and live.

CHAPTER SEVEN

"The only thing worse than being blind is having sight but no vision."

Helen Keller

Jackson was doing so well, in fact, that after he attained his environmental diploma he applied for several positions in his field and was successful in landing two jobs. He accepted the offer in Toronto, about an hour and a half away, because he could live with his cousin Todd.

Relief. His mental illness was behind him. We could leave it in the past. I wasn't naïve enough to believe that really, but many of his triggers were no longer staring him in the face. No more exams, no more academic pressures. His medications were working. Perhaps he could now manage and never again have to see an emergency room. In the back of my mind I wondered if he would continue with counselling, but I didn't broach the subject.

He relocated without issue and his transition into the work force seemed remarkably uneventful. He was an avid environmentalist and his new job was for a consulting company that designed and implemented systems geared to minimize damage to our environment. He was doing work that would have direct and positive impacts. He'd earn a steady income and let go of the stressors that came with academia.

Before we knew it, it had been almost a full year since he'd graduated and moved to Toronto. He'd had some highs and lows with his mental health but was managing them quite well. He had started dating a girl named Jade and seemed genuinely content. We thought the worst was behind us.

Annually, we all three travel to Florida for ten days of winter vacation. Jackson's return tickets had been purchased, and we planned to pick him up at the airport in Sarasota. He didn't make a phone call to us, but for two days during our drive south, Jackson's text messages from Ontario were clear indications that he was in a bad place:

I wonder if I should ask for a higher limit on my credit card.

I should get a puppy.

I'm going off meds.

I wanna learn to play the drums.

I wondered if part of his apparent anxiety was triggered by his impending flight two days later. He would have been travelling alone, which he has done in the past without issue. I am not a psychologist; my degree is in business. He was clearly looking for external gratification, just as he had with alcohol. These things were "outside" fixes that might make him feel better for short periods of time, but some could be disastrous.

What had set all of this in motion?

As we waited at the airport in Sarasota and saw him coming down the escalator, we were taken aback. Our usually immaculate, particular son was dressed in big baggy track pants and a sweatshirt, his long, dirty-blond hair pulled back into a ponytail. As he got closer to us, I could see his ashen face and bloodshot eyes while his chewed fingernails shone out to me like a beacon of his inner turmoil.

The signs were clear—he was on the brink of breakdown. Craig and I were so scared we did not know what to say as we glanced into each other's faces. We were both speechless and worried about saying the wrong thing, especially in public.

I felt my knees begin to buckle and held onto the railing of the bench I had been sitting on. We welcomed Jackson, each with a hug, while trying desperately to mask our true feelings as we walked toward the car in the parking lot.

It was very clear to Craig and me that eating had been an issue. We had not seen Jackson for two months, and his weight loss was very apparent. He said that he had not been eating well and had recurring diarrhea. Diet, brushing your hair, having a shower, exercising…it's all about taking care of ourselves. When Jackson was in one of his states, he wasn't thinking about himself or even caring about the basics.

On the way to the rental home, we stopped at the grocery store. We weren't sure if he would shop with us, but he did. He agreed only to cereal and 2% milk. We picked up some other things, including protein bars and fresh fruit in hopes that he might change his mind.

Craig and I tried to lighten things up so we could all enjoy our time together. We agreed we would re-implement his safety plan. We did not impose ourselves by asking too many questions and decided to be patient and wait for him to share what he wanted to, when he wanted to.

I hope to God he never again finds himself in that state.

Sarasota, Sunshine. Self-care or more bull? I didn't know. Should I go? I couldn't. I could barely get out of bed to go to work. Why did this happen to me? I didn't even want to eat. I couldn't pull myself out of it.

Maybe the way I was feeling was because of my meds. Were the pills controlling me and my moods? Did they need to be adjusted? Sunshine and sleep. Mom would do everything for me, and maybe we could all have some fun and chill. No work stresses. No Jade insulting me or screaming insults. Without her going off the deep end all the time, I might have been able to relax. If she called me a lot, I could turn off my phone. I needed to get my head back on straight. Jade had taken everything I had—sucked it out of me.

Run away. I needed to get out of there.

Things changed quickly that evening, when Jackson called his father from the bedroom in which he was using one of two single beds. There was something in the tone of his voice that made me follow my husband.

As Craig pushed open the door, we were aghast. We'd thought Jackson had crawled into bed to talk to his girlfriend, do some gaming, and relax. But he was in the dark, wrapped in a blanket and hugging a pillow crying, "I want to die. I can't handle this anymore." He started rocking back and forth and threw his pillow across the room, knocking over a lamp. He then reached down under the covers and lifted his right hand, holding a razor blade between his fingers. He screamed, "Let me in the bathroom," trying to push by, yelling that he needed the blade.

Craig got between Jackson and the door, blocking him. Jackson dropped the razor blade and struck at his father, eventually collapsing to the floor.

I was crying, lost. How were we supposed to respond?

Not knowing what to do, we sat on the bed with him, telling him how much we loved him and that he would get through this. We were there and nothing was going to hurt him.

After some time, exhaustion took over and Jackson fell asleep. He was safe. We weren't going anywhere. We stayed with him through the night. Craig sat in the reclining chair, while I took the additional single bed beside our boy. He got through. I got through. Craig got through.

I knew if I cut my wrists, it would kill my pain. I would bleed out slowly, listening to my parents' voices in the other room. But I couldn't do that to them. What would they do when they found me? They wouldn't understand. They would blame themselves. I couldn't have that. It wasn't their fault. It was mine. What could I do about all that shit that kept getting dumped on me?

There had to be an answer...A way to battle through...I couldn't do this to them.

How did a parent do this? How were we supposed to function daily, wondering what our child was going to do next? Would he be happy or distraught? When I walked into the room, what was I going to find? How would he be? What would we have to do?

Again, what was real and what was not? I didn't know what to believe anymore. I did know that regardless, he was a mess. We searched his room and took away anything he might use to harm himself and I slept in the bed beside him again the second night. He was much more stable or so it seemed.

Big strides did happen—we spoke openly about marijuana and binge drinking. Jackson described it as best he could. Smoking up started as a way for him to avoid panic attacks. It made him feel totally relaxed, almost euphoric at first.

I'd thought I had been a confidant, but he had kept these secrets to himself. I was shocked, upset and felt betrayed. I had been foolish to think that he shared almost everything with me, but he had been using marijuana since he was a teenager! Right in our community, pretty much before our eyes and we had been oblivious.

I was angry and left Craig in charge to go for a walk. I wanted to scream at Jackson. What was he thinking? We could have gotten him help years ago! If we had known, would things be different today? Why didn't he tell us? Who else knew?

A piece to the puzzle—he'd started smoking up when I was facing breast cancer. Oh my God.

In addition to speaking about his challenges, he began putting his phone on silent mode during the day, by choice. The conversations with his girlfriend seemed matter of fact—odd for two people who believed they were falling in love. Jackson was unhealthy in many ways and sought external validation for so much. He was battling within himself.

What I wanted for our son…happiness, confidence in himself, a sense of fulfillment and the strength to manage his mental illness. He was making some positive choices but had stopped counselling when he moved to Toronto. He said he thought it had helped in London, but that he hadn't really connected with the psychologist. I wasn't even sure if he was still taking his medications.

Jackson had refused to seek out any support groups—or even just pairing up with someone his age. He blamed his anxiety. I couldn't understand as I was not walking in his shoes. There were hundreds of young adults struggling as he was. I hoped he could connect with someone as a confidant; someone who "got it" because they lived it.

I asked him what he thought his triggers had been the week before. He said it was his job. I held my composure, replying that I thought there might be multiple factors. Alcohol? Girlfriend? All was fine there, he told us. But I had watched him read texts and immediately get upset, roll his eyes, walk away, or laugh.

It wasn't my business, but when it came down to his happiness, I could not ignore it. He was very guarded, sharing little about the texts he was reading, but his comments and nonverbal signals said it all. I don't think his girlfriend had any understanding of his mental health. She worked in a retail store at one of the local malls and seemed to have wonderful people skills. But when he was feeling low and just wanted time to himself, she didn't understand. She imposed herself rather than giving him the time he needed. She passed judgment rather than seeking to at least accept his struggles.

His triggers were clear to me; academia, crowds, public speaking, relationships, the unknown. He misinterpreted, reacted, acted impulsively and sought validation in unhealthy ways. But Craig and I couldn't be the ones giving him affirmation. Our fear was that he would have short-term satisfaction, and then believe he was doing fine, which was a recurring problem.

He is twenty-five, June, I said to myself. He must own this. He must make the decisions. You couldn't convince him of anything even if you wanted to.

One might wonder why we didn't take him to the hospital that first night. We didn't even follow his safety plan. Perhaps it was the history of hospital visits. Each time, almost every time, they held him overnight to ensure he was "stabilized." He might speak with a psychiatrist and he might get a referral. Then they called him a cab if he went on his own and didn't have a ride home. During this crisis in Florida, we firmly believed that keeping him there with us was the best decision. He would stabilize, but with us.

We wanted to make every day as wonderful as it could possibly be and tackle one big item each day. Our hope was that by the end of the week, he'd be in a good place with a firm plan for his future.

Love and hope—that's all the power we had.

CHAPTER EIGHT

"All human unhappiness comes from not facing reality, squarely, exactly as it is."

Buddha

How misguided we were. We had a few great days, golfing, lounging on the beach, and cheering on the Baltimore Orioles at a spring-training game. The crisis passed…until Jackson called out from his room, again.

I paused before I entered the door, hesitant and scared. As I went in, he was sobbing, holding a handful of his pills and muttering that he'd spit them out. What had happened? What had caused this change? What was the trigger? I hugged him from behind as Craig rushed in and took the pills away from our son. Jackson slowly calmed and he agreed; we needed to take him for help. We called the insurance company, who directed us to the nearest hospital with an emergency department serving mental health. He said nothing on the way to the hospital, just staring out the window, sitting beside me in the back seat. I couldn't take my eyes off him.

After triage and about an hour's wait, he was admitted for bloodwork and a urine test, several interviews with nurses, and a "work up." Under Florida's "Bakers Act," he was not allowed to leave. We learned that he met the established criteria to be held involuntarily for up to seventy-two hours. He was being held in a hospital gown, in a room clearly set up for at risk patients. There were no machines, no shelves, no medical materials—nothing but the bed. We understood that he would be transferred to a mental-health facility by ambulance sometime in the night.

We had all his things, including his cell phone. Upset and with no answers at about two-thirty in the morning, Craig and I argued in the parking lot, after we were told we could not stay with him.

"Are you kidding me? We can't be with our son? Not even one of us? How can we walk away and leave him like this?" Craig was calm and rational as I yelled at him. In my mind, we were deserting Jackson.

On the way to the rental home I continued to vent, angry and fearful—where would he be sent? How long would he be there? What services would he need? When would we know? Why didn't we think to take the pills out of his room?

When our heads hit the pillows we were out, exhausted from our emotions, worry, and questions—until six a.m. when we got a call. He was being moved to a behavioural clinic. We would be contacted later to hear more.

Failure. How could my little boy be on a seventy-two-hour hold in a mental health facility? Guilt. That's what I bore. On the other hand, that day was peaceful, almost refreshing in some ways. How could I feel that way when I knew where he was? Because we had his phone. Because I wasn't perseverating on what his state of mind was. Because he couldn't text me or call. Because he was in good hands with professionals who were experts in what they did. Yes, we swam, walked, drank tons of coffee—all the while waiting patiently for a phone call from Jackson or a clinician.

Things changed when we went to visit that evening at six p.m. The facility itself was the oldest in the area. When we finally found the entrance, the door was secured, requiring us to buzz for entry. We waited. A security guard asked us to sign in and leave all our belongings in a locker. He then used a handheld metal detector, scanning each of us. I hated being treated this way and thought I was going to be physically sick. What would happen next? Would we even be allowed in to see our son? It seemed to be taking so long. I sat down in a chair as we waited to enter through another bolted door which lead to a large open area with several circular tables. Many staff members were working at desks on the other side of break-proof windows.

Jackson had been waiting, immediately joining us in one of the four chairs. No hugs, no slap fives, no greetings. He announced that they were letting him go. He had seen the psychiatrist and he was leaving. Period.

Really?

He disclosed that it was all much clearer but would not elaborate. He didn't need to worry about work now because he was in a psych ward. They couldn't penalize him for taking more time off for vacation.

What progress had he made though? He had told them he did not want to die. But there was so much more. He had been admitted to what was a frightening place. All around us we saw people who were clearly ill—one hallucinating. Was my son just as ill?

One man towered over everyone, maintained a stern expression, and stood confidently with his arms crossed in front of him, radio clipped to the front of his shirt. He was one of the three security staff standing guard during visiting hour.

Jackson pleaded with us to get him out of there. The bathroom had urinals, toilets, and showers—all open without any curtains or doors for privacy.

His actions warranted this response because they must keep everyone safe, we explained.

He shared that they had made him go to a support group meeting and asked each participant to share five goals. How horrible—in his mind. A waste of time.

We pushed by asking what his plan was.

He totally deflected the question and said he was going to sit by the pool at the rental home and do some gaming.

Excuse me? We were asking about his wellbeing, not his vacation.

He continued to share that he didn't need to go home as soon as he was released. He could stay in Sarasota, because he had a medical note excusing him from work.

I was about to jump across the table. Instead we pushed him on a few things…the use of drugs and alcohol. When you start something that you think will help, but drop it shortly thereafter—what does that mean? It's a pattern of behaviour.

The clock seemed to stop when Jackson said that therapy was a waste of time. That's when Craig did what he does best—he got to the point. "You're here, in a mental-health facility because you were trying kill yourself. You want to leave after less than a day? You won't go to therapy, and you think we should just get in the car and carry on with our vacation?"

Jackson's face said it all—total denial. Or was this his way of maintaining control?

By the end of the hour, we knew that they had decided to change his medication. A nurse joined us at the table to inform Jackson that he was not being released. Craig and I were treated like bystanders. I thought Jackson might have a breakdown over this, but he maintained his composure. We saw the tough side of our son in that moment. I hugged him for what seemed like an eternity. I couldn't let go. What were we leaving him to?

There were no other visitors left as the guard walked towards us. Regardless of how I felt, we were being forced to leave.

The bottom line was that Jackson was twenty-five. We didn't even get to talk to the clinician and were told we wouldn't be. They don't talk to parents in an adult ward. We couldn't release him even if we wanted to, which took a great deal of pressure away from us, but at the same time made us feel a total loss of control. We held on to what we could and went shopping. He needed clean clothes—nothing with drawstrings, no sleeveless muscle shirts, no belts, no shorts, no shoes with laces.

I was so afraid for him. What was going to happen to him in there? What would he be exposed to? Would this experience increase his anxiety (which he clearly had, without question)? Would it cause trauma, or cause him to rethink and never threaten suicide again?

It was never a conscious choice, June. When someone is suicidal, they are feuding within themselves.

I sat in a corner, the safest place I could find, so no-one could come up behind me, thinking, I hate this place. I can't believe they've forced me to be here! They shouldn't have that right. Get me out. I'm not like everyone else here. They really are sick.

People were pacing back and forth, talking to themselves. The security guards were scary enough.

I tried to stay in my room, or I should say, hide there. There was only one person sharing it with me, and he seemed OK. We didn't talk much. But they wouldn't let us stay in our rooms and didn't give us any privacy. I decided I was never taking a shower. There were no curtains. It was wide open for everyone to see. Even the toilet stalls didn't have doors. I didn't want to think about what terrible things happened there.

What could I do to get out? Should I pretend I was OK? Pretend I wasn't having the thoughts I truly was? They wouldn't even let me call my parents. Didn't I get at least one phone call?

I had to get through this day. I'd tell them anything they wanted to know to just get out of this hell hole. Maybe I was scared because it was all out of my control. I didn't know what was coming next. Who was going to see me? What were they going to make me do? I was trapped. I needed to know! It was the anxiety. I wasn't allowed a phone or access to the outside world; my thoughts were killing me. I thought about taking pills to kill myself. But I saw these people were suffering so badly. I was just trying to run away.

They forced me to do stupid activities—even a group therapy session. Six of us were seated in chairs in circle formation. I wished there was a desk or table in the middle of us. I felt like I was left wide open, prey for an attack. I hated the idea of support groups. Why would I tell strangers my feelings and secrets? Why did I need a counsellor to tell me that if I talked about it, I'd feel better? I hate counsellors, they're all the same. I always feel babied. The ones I saw as a kid and in college. The social worker in high school. You

*don't know what's best for me. You don't experience mental illness
yourself—you study us.*

*As I listened to others share though, I understood them. I had
more in common than I thought I would. I couldn't talk. The words
would not come out of my mouth, but the thoughts were in my
head. I might have been wrong. Maybe getting to know people
who had anxiety themselves could help me when I got out of there.
Maybe. For now, I was just doing my time.*

My worry the next morning was that he was going to fake
it. He was going to say what he knew they wanted him to. This
was too real. He wouldn't have a breakthrough. He needed
to work through his feelings with a qualified clinician and dig
deep to understand them and what he could do to overcome his
challenges or at least be aware of things when they happened.
Control? Self Esteem? Attention Seeking? Inability to cope? I
think these were all components, but the last one more so. He
wasn't coping with the stressors caused by his mental illness.
With the proper help, maybe he could put things in place to cause
himself to pause before acting.

If he thought this was justification to take time off work, he
likely had the documentation to do so. I would fully support his
decision…*if* he was seeking help; seeing a therapist regularly
and following the recommendations. I prayed that was his path
forward…that he could learn to identify the triggers that led to
all these behaviours.

A new sunrise, as I sat contemplating what would happen
next, preparing for so many possibilities. Would he take a flight
out and go back to Toronto or stay and come back in the car with
us? Would he get a referral to a psychiatrist in Canada again?

Stop June. You won't be the one to decide.

He would. That was the toughest part, having to sit back and
watch him continue to self-destruct. How does a parent do that?

As I grappled with how to respond properly, I knew I needed to get help for myself. I was committed to not enabling or feeding Jackson's behaviour, but I also understood his emotional highs and lows. Yet, how does one know what is real and what is not? What to respond to and what to ignore? What to redirect and what to accept?

Just after lunch, Craig called the behavioural centre for an update. Jackson was required to give his consent before they could talk to us. We were told that he would see the doctor again that day who worked in the afternoons. If Jackson gave consent, a clinician would call us back. I then called our insurance provider to make inquiries. We had purchased family medical coverage for the trip to Sarasota so had no concerns financially. Had they received any documentation from either the hospital or the centre? Nothing. The last update was my phone call to them. It seemed we would be left hanging.

Craig and I walked, swam in the pool, and read, killing time as we anxiously awaited news.

We heard nothing until we went for a visit at six p.m. Jackson immediately asked us if we had gotten a call because he was being released. We had not. Regardless, just after seven p.m. we were leaving with him. He had documentation outlining his prescriptions and a statement saying he would follow up with services in Canada.

Of course, when we asked for a briefing, the answer was clear—he's an adult. He can share what he wants with you. That certainly worked—when or if he chose to share!

We did have a laughable moment. Jackson pulled out a napkin with contact information from another young man (sitting at the table beside us with his aunt), which was written in crayon. They were not allowed to use pens or pencils. They chuckled when they told us that someone had smuggled in chocolate and was sharing it the past night before it was taken away.

I was impressed that Jackson had adjusted to this new living situation with humour. A closed-custody mental health unit was a new experience for all of us.

He insisted on going back to Toronto, which was surprising after what he'd said the day before. But we had no control. It was his decision. We changed his return flight to the following night. His girlfriend, Jade, had agreed to meet him, and his cousin would be at the apartment. He had a doctor's appointment that Friday morning, and it was too important to miss. He needed new prescription orders (they'd only given him three days for each) and a referral to a psychiatrist. We were calm, composed, and celebrating these coping skills. He needed to believe in himself.

That night, he slept like a prince. We snuck in often during the night to check on him. He had promised he would never attempt to overdose again. Although I wanted to sleep in the extra bed again, I did not—Craig and I crept in and out of his room throughout the night instead, spelling each other off to get some broken sleep, however impossible that was.

I felt calm, hopeful. Why? I don't really know except there were indications that he was in a much better place. But I didn't want him to go back to Toronto where I had no idea what was happening.

At the same time, though, he had made the choice and we needed to respect it and support him. I wanted to ask him questions to prepare him for his arrival in Toronto. But what I wanted to do was not what should have been done. I had to back away. The controlling mom in me was the roadblock. The protector. The matriarch. The overseer. That was my problem, not his.

Craig and I agreed that we needed help learning how to deal with this. We saw things from different sides of the fence, which had been causing tension in our marriage for some time. It would be a priority for us after our return to London.

We had a full day with Jackson before dropping him off at the airport Thursday evening. We hung out around the pool, went to his favourite restaurant for lunch, and did some last-minute shopping. He really did not speak much about his last few days but occasionally shared some information.

Soon he was back in Toronto. I endeavoured not to become a "creeper" on social media, but I was apprehensive about the transition time. He had new medications, one of which could increase suicidal tendencies. He needed to be monitored, but again, I didn't have the right to enforce that.

Craig and I agreed we were going to enjoy our last day in Sarasota, playing eighteen holes of golf followed by a delicious seafood meal seated on an outdoor balcony. The gentle sound of the waves crashed against the shoreline as we relished the bold and brilliant sunset over the Gulf of Mexico. We clinked our wine glasses together in silence, praying for our son's well-being.

Northbound on our trip home, reality smacked us in the face. Thanks, but no thanks. In some ways, I would have rather been living in my fantasy world.

How many times does a mother have to be slapped across the face to see the clear signs that are right in front of her? A friend of mine had told me for some time that Jackson wasn't showing empathy. No empathy? Our son had always been wonderful with children. He loved animals and was truly affectionate with our current family cat, Maxine. I had seen him reach out to friends in need, many times. How dare she say that? I defended Jackson and told her she had no idea what she was talking about. Why couldn't I see it myself? I should have listened to her. I had been in denial, living in the past. Jackson was no longer a child. When his mental health deteriorated, it surely put an enormous strain on his well-being. She saw signs that I was blind to. He had put up protective barriers. I knew my son was kind and caring but not everyone saw that side of him. From my friend's perspective, Jackson had become a different person.

There had been additional considerations to his earlier diagnosis of anxiety. Depression, a Borderline Personality Disorder[4]... As a parent, I detested the word, "disorder" for many reasons. In this society, even though things have been evolving, it's not a term that is welcomed. When someone is labelled as having a "disorder" the focus becomes negative. Wouldn't it be wonderful if we could celebrate people despite their circumstances, without judgment?

From our understanding, anxiety continued to be the only thing that had been formally diagnosed. The label helped us understand the specifics of how Jackson and our family could move forward, but in the end, was that what was most important?

CHAPTER NINE

"These mountains that you are carrying, you were only supposed to climb."

Najwa Zebian

When would be the next crisis? In five minutes, today, tomorrow? It was only a matter of time.

Craig and I arrived home after two days of driving. Jackson and I had already agreed that I would drive up to Toronto to spend an afternoon with him upon our return.

I left London around one-thirty due to an ice storm, waiting until after the temperature had risen to two degrees Celsius. It poured all the way, flipping to freezing rain through Woodstock. Five and a half hours later, I arrived, and it was clear the couch would become my bed for the night. There was no way I could drive home safely, as I was exhausted.

I treated Jackson to Kelsey's restaurant and listened as he shared his thoughts. It was a relief to have him to myself. There had been many baby steps, but I was disconcerted by some things he would confess over the course of the night.

After dinner Jackson and I sat up for a couple of hours talking about anything that came up. Craig and I had talked to Jackson about using cannabis oil for the anxiety. In Florida we had been stunned to learn that he had started using pot in high school. And, of course, the drinking had become a nightmare for a short period of time. How could we not have seen his distress?

As I sat in shock listening to more revelations, I felt intensely guilty. Why had he chosen not to speak to us about these things? He clearly confided in friends and they remained loyal to those secrets. But as a result, he had not gotten any help in dealing with what I am sure was trauma. He thought things were his fault and getting high became a release. While he did not say much about my illness, that time period was indeed traumatic. It was part of the puzzle.

We then had an open conversation about personality disorders, which typically develop in teenage years or early adulthood. There are many different types, but when Jackson had first started counselling, the psychologist openly discussed this as a possible diagnosis.

Childhood trauma is one possible cause. Jackson had a childhood full of enriching experiences, but he also had health issues and extreme emotional outbursts at home. It had been a difficult birth and at four months of age he'd been afflicted with some type of virus in his lungs. Ventolin treatments at home followed. As time progressed, he was confirmed to have asthma.

A particularly traumatizing event happened when he was three years old. Jackson was being transferred from a clinic to a hospital by ambulance. Another child was also being taken with his mother, who had no transportation. I was not allowed to be with them. By the time I arrived, my son was hysterical. They were trying to give him an IV and despite my attempts to console my distraught child, I could not. I was far too upset myself. A nurse then abruptly took him from me, insisting they needed to take him to a different room. I followed, but regrettably, did not go through the door. Jackson continued to cry, calling for me. They carried him back to me with the IV in place and his arm immobilized, wrapped in what seemed to be a type of block. I held him for a long time until we could both lie down on the hospital bed together. When Craig arrived, he was fit to be tied and went immediately to the nurses' station demanding to see a supervisor.

Jackson wrote about that experience as a school project, and I was shocked at how much he remembered. He became terrified of doctor visits and particularly needles/vaccines of any kind. Could these things, all of them in sequence, have been initial triggers for mental illness?

I returned home from Toronto the next night, as confident as I could be that he was safe. However, after he had answered a phone call during our dinner together, I was concerned about his girlfriend. I could see the "real" Jade through that dialogue I'd overheard. She was curt and demanding on the phone. Why wasn't Jackson with her? She was upset that he was spending time with his mother.

From what Craig and I knew, when Jade and Jackson had first started dating, she was a social butterfly. She'd introduced him to her friends, took him to events in the city, held his hand, and cuddled with him whenever she could. But then she'd begun cutting Jackson down, calling him a pathetic loser. The next minute she acted like she cared and apologized to him. She began insisting they stay at home, apart from friends and family. She controlled him. Don't do that or I'll…. Don't do this or… This young woman knew he was not well. From what he'd shared with me, he was starting to see for himself the damage she was causing. But he truly thought they were in love. He had told her about his anxiety, but she said she was protecting him, and he should toughen up and "get over it." As he questioned everything he said and did, she fed into his doubt. Would she approve? Would she break up with him?

You can't be in a relationship and only take the good that comes with it. If she had really cared about him, she would never have treated him that way. What was her intention?

With such a complex set of needs and reactionary states, Jackson would have to be totally committed to the work he would need to do…but who was I to tell him so?

During my check-in phone call that Sunday, he was upset about something that had happened at work—people cutting him down. It didn't matter who or what had happened—it was not the people around him who caused him to self-destruct. I tried to point out that he was the one who had a choice. It wasn't his girlfriend, Craig, or me. It wasn't his friends or co-workers. It was his lack of ability to respond appropriately to what many of us consider everyday occurrences. Smoking pot and drinking had previously been two of his outlets, but with guidance and support he could change how he responded to his stressors.

The next day, I found myself looking at my phone, worrying, waiting for the next text or phone call. And then I realized that if I was not healthy, how could I be there for him? I called our benefits office and scheduled a counselling session. Craig and I needed to know how to properly respond and support, so we would not enable or react inappropriately. We were desperate to understand as best as we could. In the meantime, we continued to meet on middle ground—Craig having somewhat of the opinion of, "We have to trust in him to figure it out," and me on the other side, wanting to step in to save our son.

Over the years I have recommended counselling to many friends, and each time, they have thanked me. Why didn't I follow my own advice sooner? Our first session was extremely helpful. In my mind, I knew what I had to do, but my heart was a barrier.

What we learned/affirmed:

- We can't be there for someone else if we are not well ourselves. Perseverating on what "might" happen is emotionally exhausting. We had seen the effects of the previous couple of months. I lacked the motivation to go sketch or even do my gardening. I missed appointments, was not focussed, and worked late. I constantly looked at my phone for signs that he was communicating and OK. This needed to stop. My health was suffering. And I wondered, if I had not been checking on Jackson so frequently, would my husband have been drawn in the way I had been? Had I become Craig's crutch?

- If I didn't hear from Jackson within the day, I had been "creeping" on social media to see if he posted. I'd send a text with a question, waiting for a reply. *Hi Honey. How do I tag someone on Instagram?* This wasn't for him—it was for me. I needed to know he was safe. This too had to stop. We would affirm with Jackson that he would call if he needed us and trust that he would do so, as he had almost every time. He was an adult. I was so sick of hearing that sentence. He made his own choices. He lived by them. Again, nauseating, but it was a fact. He was an adult with a possible personality disorder, and I was supposed to accept that he would make his own choices? He often did not see things rationally as he was so distraught from extreme emotions. Until he could manage that, he would continue to struggle.

- We needed to validate and affirm his emotions and actions when they were positive but NOT engage in those that were harmful or not in his best interests. We would not ask him about his girlfriend and give him the impression that we supported the relationship.

- Boundaries. We needed to set them and not negotiate. As a twenty-five-year-old, he would no longer get to raise his voice at us. He did have extreme outbursts sometimes, taking little or no responsibility for his own actions, and often blamed others. He constantly looked for external reinforcement but had yet to begin the real work in therapy. The advice was to never speak in absolutes. If, for example, we said he could not come home unless he started counselling, that would be an absolute line in the sand. What would we do if he were being released from a hospital again—lock the doors? I thought not.

- When he called in a panic, we would model mindfulness, recognizing his feelings without judgment while deep breathing and remaining calm. Mindfulness is one of the modalities for several therapies.

- Expect lows. When there were long periods of time when he was well, we were so much calmer and content. But it would only be a matter of time. The triggers varied and were hard to predict—except one; final exams during each semester had been extremely stressful times for him. Thankfully, those were in the history books.

The counsellor sent us excellent articles and a video which Craig and I watched together. We had three more sessions approved as we moved through the weeks, expecting pushback from Jackson. This was not going to be easy.

For the first time in quite a while, I went out with five friends for dinner and a movie afterward. I made a point of not talking about Jackson with the group—I just tried to have fun. And I must say, we had a blast. Did I check my phone? Yes, but not as often as I had been. That was a small step forward, but I was now cognizant and keeping myself in check.

CHAPTER TEN

"Sit with the pain until it passes, and you will be calmer for the next one."

Naval Ravicant

Why couldn't they just leave me alone? Jade, my boss, my room-mates…all of them. Everybody always wanted something from me. "Can you come into work early tomorrow?" "Why wasn't this done on time?" "How come you're going for a run at night? You're ignor-ing me." "You're an asshole." I couldn't stand it. Why can't they just screw off?

I couldn't hide from Jade. She barged in whenever she wanted. She didn't even call or text first—just showed up. I never got any time to myself. Then it was all about what she wanted to do. I didn't get any say anymore. It was easier to just roll with it, but Jade made me feel like shit. I couldn't wait until she left. Peace—for a little while anyway. I didn't know how much more I could take. Vodka. Just one, or two shots, would it hurt?

Caught myself today. Would my son hurt himself? I was very aware of how my fears were controlling my thoughts. He sounded stable on the phone for our weekly call and said he hoped to get therapy started, making that statement without any prompting from us.

Hallelujah!

We hung up feeling quite reassured, but we never know if what we see or hear is real. I asked how things were with his girlfriend. Why did I do that? Not for him, but for me. I broke one of my rules. They are fine—for now anyway. But still, I should not have even broached the subject.

He was going to work without issue, he said. When I men-tioned what a great step that was and suggested he celebrate, he said the new meds made him tired. But they don't seem to be keeping him in bed for hours or days.

I really had no idea how depleting this was. It's true what they say—it's always easier when we are on the outside looking in. My mind told me what I should have been doing, and I didn't listen. I had a vision of whacking myself on the side of the head, still creeping on social media to see if he had posted anything or messaging him to help me learn how to do something. I knew why. I hoped that the ongoing counselling sessions would help me see beyond that, but I highly doubted it. I was a mom, plain and simple. Whatever I could do for Jackson I would, even if it was to my own detriment. My child was more important to me than my own life.

Counselling session 2:

Again, affirmation that this was never going to be easy. Jackson's highs and lows would continue. However, we were very relieved. Our counsellor said that Jackson was in a much better place than he could be. She pointed out that he could articulate why he used marijuana, was able to identify traumatic events that occurred in his life, and that he reached out when in crisis.

That was a wonderful perspective. When Jackson began counselling again, he would have a good foundation to begin from. Awesome.

In terms of myself, we confirmed my boundaries. I shared that I would not talk to Jackson about his girlfriend, and the counsellor verified that this was what I needed to do. I admitted that I still crept on social media because I needed to know he was OK.

The counsellor asked Craig and me to set personal goals. Jackson had always called when he was in crisis. We needed to trust that he would continue to do so and relax. That was so darn easy to say, but not to live.

◆◆◆

I owned my actions and decisions. I broke one of my main guidelines—again. Jackson then hated me. That's the way a phone call ended as he screamed at me. I had told him what I thought about Jade...all of it! "She's poisonous...She only cares about herself...

Look at the way she treats you! You deserve so much more…
Imagine being with someone who lifts you up, makes you feel
amazing every day…You need to dump her. She's a narcissist."

I was the one who'd spoken out of line and pushed him to
react. Waiting for him to contact me was the best strategy. He
likely needed time. He avoided me and I was eating myself up
inside. I hoped he would realize that I only wanted what was best
for him.

Then Jackson called me about a totally different topic. He
was going to get a new phone and phone number—tired of all
these people who say they are friends when they are not. A fresh
start was never a bad idea, but I wondered what the catalyst had
been…probably a mood flip.

If I had been graded for those two weeks, it would be a failing
mark. Try as I might, I just couldn't do as I was told. I couldn't just
sit back and watch him flounder in ways that did harm to himself.

The week that followed was quite unbelievable. Twice he
called me and then raised his voice or even yelled. Twice I had to
say that I was here for him, but I wouldn't be yelled at. Both calls
ended that way. I gave him time and eventually we reconnected.

One call was about how he was invited to take a ticket for a
concert in Ottawa and join a group because a friend had backed
out. He wanted my opinion. I did not give one but asked him
to name the pros and the cons. He pushed back, wanting me to
make the decision. I suggested that he take some time to think
about it as he had a few hours to decide.

He stayed behind. What a feeling! He had reached out asking
for advice and I had not given him an answer! He'd made the
choice on his own. That was a huge step forward for both of us.

One morning he texted me saying he didn't want to live
anymore. I took some time to formulate a response. He was not
suicidal; I chose to believe. He had always called me in a crisis. I

wanted to type, "What do you think you should do about that?"
but I expected an answer I didn't want to read.

Instead, I asked if he should go to the mental health crisis
centre that he knows is open. His reply…*I have to go to work.*

That was the end of the string of communication.

Did I worry? Darn right. But he said he was going to work,
which to me, meant he had a plan and was not going to self-harm.

We had standing phone calls every Sunday night. That Sunday,
he did not answer. The next day, Monday, he was not available.
The next day we connected, and he was immediately snitty. He
had texted earlier that he was taking a few days off work but that
he was fine and was hoping not to get fired. Clearly something
had happened. Had he called in sick when he was not ill?

We chose not to ask. He would share if he chose to. Forgive
us as parents for caring about whether he was losing his employ-
ment and his physical/emotional health.

Flip side—clearly, he was taking care of himself in many ways.
He was making decisions, whether we agreed or disagreed. I
was proud that I was starting to respond as I should. I no longer
told him what he should do but asked questions to guide him
in making his own decisions. I think the snitty responses were
because he had to do the work himself. He'd rather have had the
answer handed to him.

So, let's look at this in as positive a way as possible, I told
myself. I had to apply my own mindset for myself to him. He had
not quit work. He had taken a few days off. He was entitled to
take time off for medical reasons. He was making money. He was
taking his meds.

That was reassuring.

Perhaps it was time I enjoyed the wave while it was high and
celebrate all that he had accomplished. I kept getting pulled back
into the worry, because I believed he would not be well without
professional help.

Tracey, someone I once worked with had a daughter with a formal diagnosis of Borderline Personality Disorder. I had discovered this haphazardly at a breakfast meet-up. I loved the perspective shared with Tracey by her own counsellor; "Hold on to the palm tree because the tsunami is coming." It was cathartic to meet with another mother who'd had similar experiences, although different. Her daughter was now in her late thirties, had sought treatment, and was on medication that was working for her. It was a long road for them to get there, and Tracey had struggled as I was…desperately wanting to help yet pushed away.

It gave me hope. Tracey and I spoke at length about what she had discovered in her own counselling sessions; her change in mindset and outlook. She had also become involved in a support group offered by Parents for Children's Mental Health. There are chapters across the province and one right here in London. I was more comfortable speaking directly with one qualified person. But there was comfort in knowing that there was another possibility and that other parents were facing the same challenges.

Jackson unexpectedly drove home one afternoon planning on visiting for the weekend. I wasn't sure what had happened, all I knew was what he shared. Apparently, he'd gone back to work but had a panic attack in his car. When he'd calmed down enough, he drove to the clinic and so had a medical note to be off work.

By the time he got home to us, he was in good spirits. He joined Craig and me for dinner and hung out with some buddies for the night. Friends in tough times can bring a healing touch, especially if they help you to laugh. I hoped he was enjoying himself.

As I tried to get into the mind of someone with a mental illness, I saw the emotional highs and lows. I saw the trigger, or series of triggers. I saw Jackson floundering for acceptance. Perhaps something else had happened with Jade, but I wasn't going to ask. Was that why he wanted a new phone number?

Hold on. When he came home he suggested that he needed to take an extended leave from work and asked if he could stay home for a while. There were too many stressors in Toronto that he needed to take a break from, including Jade.

Wow! That was a lot to take in. Jackson had talked to the doctor at the clinic, who supported an extension of his absence. He was looking at options and needed to decide before an appointment next Tuesday.

Taken aback, Craig and I needed to have a full discussion. How would we deal with this? We would absolutely welcome Jackson home for a little while as he worked through this, but what boundaries would we set? We were all over the place, but after a long talk agreed on some possible ground rules we could both live with.

We were able to move our counselling session ahead. What might it look like with Jackson being home? What should we set as expectations? How would we draw those boundaries 24/7? How would we stay well and balanced?

- A Safety Plan would be in place while he was staying with us.
- We expected him to follow through with the referral for med reviews and counselling he received in Florida. We would not make it non-negotiable because I knew for a fact we would never kick him out should he return to the hospital. Tough parenting, I can only do to a point.
- Mutual respect meant we would let him know when we would be away or late and expect the same of him.
- He would act as an adult living in our home—meaning he'd clean up after himself and help. We should not have to ask for things to be done. He should just step in when he saw the need.

- He was on his own financially. Although, he was still paying his rent in Toronto, so we wouldn't be charging him at home.
- We would not be yelled at. We would walk away and engage in the conversation when he was able to do so reasonably.
- We would respect his personal space as he would respect ours.

Jackson's room was in an area of the house that was fairly private. He had his own living space with a microwave, a small fridge and a washroom. He had access to our full kitchen when he needed it. The uncertainty of what this would look like over time was discomforting. We were anticipating a month, but really had no idea.

I looked forward to getting him settled. I'm sure he did as well. He was growing frustrated with the down time.

Sounds perfect doesn't it? Enter mental health.

◆◆◆

Farewell to reason. I had walked away from him several times already. When he raised his voice or became curt, I left the room. I was clear that I would not engage in that kind of conversation.

Stress times one hundred. I was on eggshells—all the time now.

One day we were on our way to pick up a couple of things, and he was over-the-top angry and yelling at me. I pulled into a parking lot, turned around, and headed back home. He asked what I was doing. I told him I would not be spending any time with him while he behaved this way. I had hoped for an enjoyable afternoon with him but I would not be yelled at. He changed his tone quite quickly.

What was the trigger? Which one this time? A text from Jade.

We went over things with our counsellor and had to continue to change our way of thinking. He wasn't a child anymore. If I thought of it as though he was living in his own space, his coming and goings—it made it easier. It was all his business. I didn't need to get worked up about things, because I chose not to need to know. He'd be joining us for dinners now and then, and had full access to the house, of course—but this would really be best for everyone. We had to find a way to not react when he pushed our buttons. He didn't even know when he was pushing them some of the time.

It was the decisions. They were reactional, nonsensical sometimes. But I didn't own them. How could we expect it to change when he really thought everything was just fine?

CHAPTER ELEVEN

"The pen that writes your life story must be held in your own hand."

Irene C. Kassorla

What was wrong with them? Didn't they get that I needed to run? I came home to get away from Jade and all the other shit that was happening. I was having trouble getting out of bed again and couldn't figure out why. It just happened. I couldn't do anything about it. A day or two was all I needed and then I forced myself up and out. Off we went again.

I really loved my work, especially when I could be alone and figure out a solution to a problem no one else could. But I was calling in sick too much. They didn't get it. They probably thought I was lazy like Jade did. I wondered if I should I tell them about my anxiety.

I found this amazing marathon over in Belgium that sounded cool. I just needed a little loan from Mom and Dad, but they wouldn't give it to me. Why not? They always helped me out when I needed it before. What was different this time?

It would have been so great to take off for a week. They said I was running away. Damn right I was. If I wasn't around I didn't have to talk to anyone. I didn't have to fight to leave the apartment. I'd be fine in a place where no one knew me. I was a great runner and that was all I'd need. Why wouldn't they just let me go? It was only a break. I knew what would be waiting for me when I got back.

Then we had the day of all days. It had to come. It had to happen. It was just a matter of when. On the Friday night, Jackson texted me asking for a loan of $700. Craig and I talked about it and told him that we had full confidence in his ability to find a solution of his own. It seemed that he now wanted to register and travel to run a marathon in Brussels. He did not have all the money at his disposal and registration was open. Did we know he needed to book a flight and there were additional living costs and meals?

Next day, he continued to ask. We continued to decline. He was an adult with a full-time job, and we affirmed that if he really wanted this, he would find a way. He reacted, yelled, demanded, and declined the invitation to sit down and have a rational conversation.

Craig said something that got me nervous—he was having second thoughts and wished that we had picked something else to say, "No" to. We talked before Jackson came home and agreed that we had to stick with what we decided the night before. If we gave him the money, he would again be jumping into something that took him away from doing the real work. Running was cathartic for him, no question. But giving him the money to go to a marathon on the other side of the world amid his turmoil…

When Jackson got home we attempted to redirect him to one of the countless marathons held in Ontario. We were striving to help him recognize that this was another example of not responding to stressors in a healthy way. He yelled that this meant the world to him and that he couldn't believe we wouldn't help. Try as we might, he could not see that it was about so much more than the money. We shared a couple of examples—last year it had been an all-inclusive vacation. Prior to that, it was going back to school for an additional diploma, which was surprising because he knew all too well that academia was a trigger. He did not follow up with either.

He didn't have the ability to see the big picture at the moment. He was not well—plain and simple.

Didn't we know he needed this for his mental health? he asked. When he said we had always helped before, that's when I stepped in to say yes and we should not have. "You continue to make decisions for external gratification rather than getting down to what your stressor/trauma is and learning what to do about it."

"I'm going to find another way to get the money. I'm not going to therapy either," he yelled as he stormed out. The last thing he did was text me that he was going to get drunk…and goodbye.

I was proud that Craig and I had stood together and did not back down. Jackson was attempting to manipulate us with threats, and we were not engaging. It was as though the window had opened and I'd finally seen the light!

Unsure of what to expect, we went over to our friends' house. I predicted Jackson would call, saying he needed to go to the hospital. I smiled, pretending to care about the conversation. Occasionally, I'd pull myself back in, realizing I had no idea what had just been said. I was perseverating on Jackson and what could be happening, when he would call or how we would excuse ourselves. I was certain we were headed for a crisis and afraid that our decision to not give him money was going to push him over the edge. He never called. He wasn't home when we returned. By seven p.m. the next day we still had not heard from him. I paced, sketched, went for a car ride, made a huge dinner — anything I could do to keep busy. Was he making a point? Trying to punish us? Or did he carry through with his threat and get drunk again? I chose to believe, for my own sanity, that he would stay away for a couple of days and then appear.

He'd said he wouldn't start therapy. Was that a heated moment or a valid threat? He was not thinking rationally. Had he started binge drinking again and was passed out somewhere? What if he was in a hospital? What if he was having suicidal thoughts again? Stop. I couldn't let my mind go there or to all of the other worse possibilities.

We had drawn a line and we needed to stick with it. We were supporting him despite the stress and conflict. We couldn't change our minds, otherwise we were enabling him and his poor decisions. Whatever he jumped into next, in a few months' time, he'd likely lose interest, find something else that called his name—and drop this "dream" as he had so many other times. These were not long-term solutions.

I was so much more relaxed when he was not home. Was that wrong? Should I have felt guilty? It was just that we never knew what was coming next. We had another counselling session the next week and the timing was just right. We needed some guidance going forward. I was most excited about an eight-week course I was to start the next Wednesday night—beginner's meditation. I knew that I needed tools for myself to keep me grounded, calm, and healthy.

Jackson showed up two days later with a friend. A word here. A word there. Then off he went again, saying he was going out.

What he didn't see was that he was only punishing himself. His actions, repeatedly, were unhealthy in so many ways. Yet, I couldn't begin to help him see that. I didn't know anything. He was only going to be able to see that himself. I was so afraid he would turn to alcohol again as a coping mechanism.

Couldn't we just take him back to the age of ten? If I could do it all over, I'd walk him through problem-solving steps at every opportunity. What were the pieces of this puzzle? What were the options? The pros and cons? What would be the best choice?

Maybe we gave him solutions too often, rather than helping him work through to find them himself, because we just wanted to de-escalate the situation. We couldn't go back to that time. We couldn't recreate those moments. We couldn't rewrite the psychological assessment he had back in grade six and change the recommendations. We couldn't go back and ask her to share the report with him.

We'd followed the psychologist's recommendations, taken him to a child counsellor taking his advice after every session. We'd ensured he was enrolled in team sports. We'd created a safe place where he could vent with no repercussions. We'd consulted with his teachers, ensuring he could have learning support when needed. Our family enjoyed countless wonderful vacations, full of love and laughter.

He had been ill as a baby and toddler—had that turned us into parents who were overly cautious? Did we ask "how high" every time he told us to jump? Listen to me, trying to convince myself that we did what we could—that this wasn't our fault. Or was it? Weren't parents supposed to be the gatekeepers for their children's health—both physically and emotionally? I don't care what anyone tells me, what their level of expertise is, I will always play the "should have, could have, would have" game in my mind. It's entirely different when it is your child. Mom guilt is deep. It hurts and no logic is going to change that.

I was bothered by the way he was treating me, but I knew I was his safe person. Was this his way of maintaining control? He didn't scream at his father. He would get upset but turned and walked away saying things under his breath. Yet, he would yell and scream at me. Craig was able to stay calm and tell his son to stop speaking to his mother that way. I appreciated that.

I was most distraught because what had started as an "anxious child," had become a formal diagnosis of "Anxiety Disorder" when Jackson was in grade twelve and then had spiralled into what it was now. I had to stop going back into the past. It wasn't helping at all.

Was he "wired" this way? Was this something that had been inevitable from birth?

He had said nothing about a counselling appointment and I was respecting his right to do so. I didn't ask any of "those" questions unless he began the conversation, which had yet to happen on this topic.

I did ask, point blank though, if he was taking drugs. He went out on Friday nights to a club where we all knew every type of drug was present. If he wanted it, it was there. Too many young men and women turned to drugs as a way of coping. But Jackson seemed upset that I would even think he would do such a thing. He always took a taxi home and we had not seen any recurrence of binge drinking yet. I hoped that he knew better from the way he was raised and from the experiences he'd had in his life. He had a strong sense of right and wrong. I'd have hung my hat on that.

Why couldn't we have a relationship where we went out and grabbed a bite to eat? Where we talked about everything and anything under the sun? We used to, up until only a few years ago. I missed that. I missed feeling calm, relaxed, comfortable, and being there for him.

He felt the same, I was sure. I knew he hadn't divulged everything to me, nor should he have. But at least our conversations had been free flowing. I didn't used to hesitate or wonder about what to say—what reaction it would cause. I sincerely hoped we found a way to get back to that. I hoped that, sometime in the future when it was right, Craig and I were asked to be part of any counselling work going forward.

As Jackson's support network, I knew that made a difference—when we knew what his goals were and what we should and should not do as he worked through the steps. Not knowing was torture. Because we didn't know if what we were doing was right for him. We were guided by what we had read, what I had discussed with another parent whose child had personality disorder, and what our own counsellor was suggesting. The most important part was missing—his input!

It appeared that he had dropped the marathon idea. He had not changed his diet as he would have had to if he were running in October. I did see that he was still running occasionally, which was another good sign.

CHAPTER TWELVE

"Do the best you can until you know better. Then when you know better, do better."

Maya Angelou

I began taking the meditation course. It was in a lovely studio with a beautiful view of the river. Ten of us gathered once a week for eight sessions. I was hoping this would help me keep calm and grounded.

After the first session, I was much better at not engaging. It took practice, but I was using those "middle ground" responses whenever I could.

"I'm sorry you feel that way."

"If that's what you want to do."

"I'm sorry, this is not a good time for me to talk about this. Can we continue later today?"

If I didn't give him anything to react to, I was less emotional and didn't get drawn in. It had only been one week and already I saw a difference. There was much more to this course than learning different ways to meditate. I wished I had made this discovery much sooner!

What a whirlwind. I was so happy when Jackson got a phone call with a cancellation for a psychiatrist the next afternoon in Toronto. He took the appointment but came home to London like a tornado—angry, yelling at us.

I had expected the appointment would be upsetting, and I was sure he'd been told things he did not want to hear. All he shared of any importance was that the psychiatrist had given him a prescription to change his medication, and that he was on a list to begin counselling.

Jackson announced he would have no part of any new meds. He said the ones he had started in Florida a few months ago made him feel exhausted all the time. Then, the kicker—he told us he had stopped taking all of them, cold turkey, over a month before. His decision had been contrary to the medical advice. He should have weaned himself off with proper guidance.

Exasperated, my blood pressure sky-rocketing, I walked away before I said something I would regret.

I had read many books, watched information videos, and had discussions with Jackson. We both agreed that we could see several traits of a personality disorder in him. I wasn't convinced this was the right conclusion, but regardless, it did give me guidelines to follow as a parent. I was getting caught up in finding the right diagnosis but why? It had already changed over time and would likely continue to change as he got older. I knew that medications alone would never be the answer, but weren't they part of the puzzle?

In my interpretation, Jackson's brain was always in high gear, always on alert. It was wired like he was in "fight" mode and anything could trigger it. It didn't mean that he couldn't change. He had to learn to practice techniques that allowed him to cope; to realize when he was being triggered and use strategies to defuse

The key was effective treatment and support. I had reviewed information from practitioners and mental health associations from around the world. Given a commitment and follow-through, people with this diagnosis could make tremendous gains in progress in only just one year of time.

For two weeks after this encounter with Jackson, I researched whatever I could to better understand and adjust. I strategically planned when I was going to discuss something with him and set it up so there really was no way for him to walk away. Craig and I offered options when there was a decision to be made so Jackson made the choice and maintained control. We were only guiding him in the right direction. It was another step.

One day, while in the car, I shared some information about a life coach[5] who specialized in trauma. I thought that if Jackson was not going to engage with a professional in the medical community, maybe this could be someone he connected to. I suggested he call for a free consultation session with this life coach.

Perhaps he could consider this from a new angle? He listened and then said it was the stupidest thing he'd ever heard of.

I felt as though I'd been kicked in the teeth. The dilemma now was what to do. If he really did decline treatment, his message to us was clear. Was this enough for us to ask him to move back to Toronto? It was torture to watch our son live in denial when the signs of his struggle were so clear. He was an adult and at some point we had to accept that there was little we could do, except be his "safe" people and sounding-boards.

He was insisting there wouldn't be therapy or a life coach. He refused to take any meds and was going back to work. He was fine and just needed a break.

Why could he not see the facts? He'd taken himself off meds despite believing that he suffered from a personality disorder and anxiety. He knew that there wasn't a single *answer*. Counselling, medications, fitness, sleep and nutrition were all components of a plan that could bring him more happiness in his life.

Perhaps he was too afraid to do the work. Too afraid to dig deep and get to the bottom of it all. Too afraid to admit that he was the one who needed to take responsibility. Too afraid to agree that his behaviour and choices were detrimental to himself and affecting many people around him. Was that what was holding him back?

From outside Jackson's bedroom door, I overheard a heated argument he was having with Jade. As he came down the hall and entered the kitchen, he announced in an impersonal way that they'd broken up. That was it. No additional information. As he poured himself a glass of water and headed out the door for a run, he seemed almost relieved and not in any way upset. Perhaps he had begun to address at least some of his pressures.

Jade was a mistake. It was hard enough to get out of bed and to work every day. I had to worry about what she thought and what she would say or do if I didn't go. She didn't understand and even said I was making it all up to get out of work. She was incredible when we first met, and I couldn't get her out of my mind. I gave her all of me, even my virginity. It was amazing at first. She kissed and hugged me all the time. I felt needed. I felt like I mattered. I should have known it was too good to be true.

She started to judge…all the time! She told me what to do, what not to do, who to hang out with. I needed someone who would understand, someone who would listen. My illness was invisible. That was the worst because she couldn't know how bad it was. If I cancelled a lunch date, I was boring. If I couldn't get out of bed, I wasn't trying hard enough. If I didn't clean up, I was a lazy loser. I had to run away. It was all I could do to get away. I didn't have the guts to face her.

The time away in Florida, as terrible as it ended up being, helped clear my head. I never wanted to end up in a place like that again. I couldn't imagine turning forty-five years old and still fighting my own thoughts. What I'd tried so far wasn't working. I had to find a way to manage this—to move on. Breaking up with Jade was one of the hardest, but the one of the best things I had ever done. I felt free again. Free to be myself with all the good and bad that comes with it. I didn't need to worry about anyone else anymore.

Why did they have to give me new prescriptions? I was so tired all the time. I wanted to live, to run again. I had to try without them and I know it was stupid to stop taking them all at once. That support group though…as much as I hated being forced into it, it made sense. Maybe it was time for me to get some help here. Maybe it was time to do what my parents had been asking me to do for so long. No one needed to know. I could just sit there and listen at first. It wouldn't be so bad. What could possibly happen? If I hated it, I'd split. I was free to make that choice. I wasn't locked up against my will. It felt kind of chill knowing I could make that choice myself!

Could he be happy if he were surrounded by people who accepted him without judgment? Could that positive energy influence his own mental health? He sat with me on the deck after returning from his run. "I'm turning in all of the medications I haven't used. I'll take them to the pharmacy before I leave."

Leave? It was like he'd just taken a paid vacation for a couple of weeks. I wanted to scream, but on the other hand, he had made a momentous decision in his favour by ending that poisonous relationship. Perhaps he could focus on himself now.

Wait.

"Forget about therapy, Mom. I don't need it. Now that she's out of my life I'll be fine."

I wondered if I should have mentioned the list of other stressors? If I should push back? But why would I knock him down when he was ready to move on? Ready to go back to work and focus on himself? I wanted to run into a forest and just let go of all that was building up. I felt the tension rising—the stress in my clenched jaw.

Walk away. Just walk away.

How did a parent do that? How could a mother do so, knowing that it was only a matter of time before her son had another emotional setback? Knowing that he did not have the coping strategies to deal with what was surely going to be coming his way? Frustrated that the tools were there to help him, but they were being refused?

I thought about what this might have looked like if my sister or I had had anxiety growing up. There had been no awareness of mental health back then. If anything, those with needs covered it up, embarrassed by what they were facing. But now it seemed that in some ways the pendulum had swung too far the other way. Jackson sometimes used his diagnosis as a crutch. He couldn't do something because he had "anxiety." He couldn't do something because…because…because.

It was the opposite of what his mindset should have been. If he had been in therapy, I knew that they would help him deal with the trauma and face each of these hurdles. He had great success when he ran the marathon in his second year of college. He'd had a plan and had begun preparing four months in advance. He set regular goals for running, diet, and exercise. He kept at it and finished with such pride.

I wished he could reflect on that and realize that he could make changes if his mind was made up. Was it easier for him to say he couldn't rather than do that work? That's what it came down to.

He had a full benefit plan so there were minimal costs associated with the help he could get. I couldn't live in his mind. I tried to, but just couldn't. Growing up in my generation and for those who came before, the mindset was typically, "Suck it up, buttercup." You were expected to deal with it, keep everything in check. If people were in distress, we didn't know about it. Depression or anxiety were never openly discussed. People sought help behind closed doors. Schools did not have supports or provide accommodations specific to mental illness. Community services were limited. But what were the repercussions?

Was Jackson's brain wired in a way that would cause him continued challenges for his whole life? Or was this a young man who didn't yet have the tools to work through what was thrown at him? Would he "outgrow" anxiety as he learned to manage and had new experiences? Would each challenge that he overcame give him the strength to move forward? I continued to try to rationalize what was happening rather than simply accept it for what it was.

There was an interesting lesson in my meditation class one week. Our coach led us through an exercise about relationships. And I realized that I couldn't own it. I couldn't own Jackson's happiness, his despair, his successes, or his challenges. Only he could. As hard as it was for me to wrap my head around—I had to. My interventions had not helped. If anything, they might have hindered. He didn't want to hear my advice. He didn't want to be questioned. He didn't want any part of what I needed to share. He got upset...as did I. When someone was giving you clear feedback that they did not want your help, you needed to step back.

CHAPTER THIRTEEN

"Whatever you do, hold on to hope. The tiniest thread will twist into an unbreakable cord. Let hope anchor you in the possibility that this is not the end of your story, that change will bring you to peaceful shores."

Author unknown

Craig and I had just returned from a week up in northern Ontario. For many years, we had rented a small cottage in the Midland area. This was one of two vacations we took each year. The region was gloriously beautiful in the summer. We had a small fishing boat, a paddle board, and a canoe at our disposal. The days weren't long enough for all we wanted to enjoy on the lake. We sipped on coffee while seated on the deck overlooking the view and enjoying the scents and sounds that nature has to offer. Truly relaxing in the mornings.

Jackson did not join us that year. There was something to be said for leaving everything behind. At home there was always something to do—work, the laundry, yard, gardens, cleaning, errands. In my mind it was always "staring you in the face." At the cottage, all that pressure went away. It was an escape I came to cherish as it really did give uninterrupted time to reflect, relax, refresh, and reconnect.

Now that we were home, my stress level was beginning to rise, but I was doing my best to keep it in check. While we had received only a few communications from Jackson in the week after he returned to Toronto, it did seem as though everything was as stable as it could be.

Craig and I were beginning to understand how to manoeuvre through this. At our latest appointment, the therapist had focussed on good news. Not that we didn't discuss challenges, but there had been a few things to celebrate if I took off my "control" hat. *I wanted* Jackson in counselling. *I wanted* him on the right meds. *I wanted* him in a relationship with someone who understood his mental health and loved and supported him in healthy ways. I was driven by what *I wanted*.

It needed to stop, but it was not that easy to shut down my own fear and doubt. My struggle continued to be knowing what I needed to do and following through. My heart got in the way.

Why couldn't I accept that I couldn't control Jackson's decisions, that he was an adult making his own choices, regardless of how detrimental they might be to him and his future.

Craig and I took a long walk to rehash everything in our heads. Jackson had had suicidal ideations. He had thought about taking his life often. Most people with suicidal thoughts do not make an attempt, but it was still very much a risk factor. When he put the pills in his mouth or was binge drinking,—he called out to us for help. He did the right thing in those moments. Yet, regardless of how hard we tried, he repeatedly refused therapy. That was the crux of it all and the most difficult to accept because it was a critical factor. With intervention and proper treatment, young adults with mental illness can be well. Jackson needed to recognize that his thoughts were not rational, it was the anxiety that was talking and driving his responses. Imagine the power he could take for himself if he stopped resisting! He owned all of it.

I had worked to identify the roles I had in my life. It is quite enlightening when you look at what each of us haphazardly do day by day, without giving it a second thought. I found as I worked through the exercises I'd learned and identified the behaviours that came with each role—one thing kept repeating itself: control.

As a wife, mother, sister, friend…I thrived on being in control. I planned, organized, and scheduled, and always took charge. The real question was why? From the time I was about nine years old, my father was rarely home because he travelled frequently with his job. My mother pretty much raised my sister and me singlehandedly. Circumstances aren't important. What matters is that I grew up with a role model who did it all herself, never counting on anyone. A woman of great pride, regardless of what was thrown at her, she made it work. Although that past was over and done with, it had affected my actions and outlook. I came to the realization that I had followed in my mother's footsteps.

Being in control had served me well in some roles…but clearly not in others.

It was not easy to change my frame of mind. I was the mother who needed to save my child. I was the mother who wanted to control the outcomes and make his decisions for him, because I did not trust he could do so himself. It took me many months to be able to recognize and openly admit that this might not have been in his best interests.

Regardless of my childhood, what drove me to want to be in such control of Jackson's life? It was the history, the extreme emotional lows. When your son needed to repeatedly go to the hospital emergency room because he had been self-injurious or having suicidal thoughts—what did you do with that? I would never have regrets about putting on my "Mom" hat and taking charge in those times. But outside of crisis, I now see that my responses on any given day may have enabled Jackson. He asked—I gave. He demanded—I caved in. He barked—I took it.

BUT as his parents we were and would always be there. We didn't need to continue to annoy him with questions.

Do you have a moment in time that will be ingrained in your memory forever? It was mid afternoon and I was sipping on a cup of coffee, enjoying the scene from the backyard patio as the squirrels chased each other on the branches of the maple tree. I had just picked up my canvas to begin sketching and the phone rang. Jackson was calling. I took three deep breaths before answering, worried about what was about to happen. My son sounded cheerful and upbeat as I exhaled with relief. "Thank you, Mom for not giving up on me. I've started going to group therapy." I jumped up, my skin tingling and tears welling up in my eyes as he continued, "I should have done this a long time ago." It was a moment of triumph, but I melted as I heard him say those words. Our son had begun to seek help, and he was admitting he had made mistakes, realizing that nothing external would *fix* him.

It had been in his hands all along. He was beginning to accept those negative emotions and take control of his mind. He knew it wouldn't be easy, but he had gotten to know people with similar struggles who understood and supported him. Hanging up the phone, I collapsed in my chair sobbing, overcome with happiness, relief, and hope.

We had great dreams for Jackson. He was beginning to find his way and he would prevail. We believed in him. He would be happy, successful, confident, and I was almost certain, a vocal advocate for others.

There are many other options today, outside of traditional medicine. Perhaps Jackson would also seek healthy alternatives. Perhaps he would surround himself with people who fed him positive energy rather than those who sucked it out of him. Perhaps this group would help him realize that he would need support for some time to come, if not for his entire life.

I was doing it, going to a group therapy session. I was scared to death and didn't know if I'd be able to do it, but I was going to give it a try. There was so much shit in my head I couldn't think straight. Maybe this would have helped. Maybe not.

The first time, I sat in the car and just watched the people going in. They looked OK. A couple of them seemed nervous, just like me. I took some deep breaths and started to walk towards the door.

No way. I couldn't do it.

But wait, the counsellor was standing right there. I could tell by the way he was dressed who he was. He said hello and I couldn't ditch it then. He knew I was there. I sat in the chair closest to the door, so I could leave whenever I wanted. That was something to hold onto.

How stupid was I to have avoided this for so long? I fit in now. I have people in my life who get me...and I get them.

There are eight of us and we've been meeting every Wednesday for about six weeks with our therapist, who leads the sessions. It's great having the same people there all the time. We have gotten to know and trust each other. I didn't say anything for the first few weeks, I just shook my head as others spoke. It took me longer to open up. But I'm not the only one who has trouble in large groups, who gets so nervous around people that I sweat. I'm not the only one who fumbles over my words, doesn't want to get out of bed, and tell the world to go to hell. Others here have also tried to solve their troubles through drinking, drugs, and even cutting themselves. We were all self-medicating; the only way we knew how to cope. Short-term fixes that could have ended in tragedy. Short-term fixes that left scarring, not only physically.

There are kids there who've been much worse off than me. One has been in a treatment program, one has spent time in jail after a night he can't remember, and another left home as a teenager and had no one to help or call. We talk about what we can't do or the shit we've been through. But we also talk about how to manage when we feel nothing, when we don't care, when nothing seems to matter.

I challenge my fears now and do my best to not let those negative thoughts take over. When they start to flood my brain, I now know what's happening, and I shut them down. I still have trouble some days; there is no magic wand to "fix me" overnight. I'm trying to take charge of what I do when I feel the symptoms coming on. I know that when I walk into a room with a crowd of people, it's going to be a problem. So, I plan. I go right to a spot where I know I'll be OK —against a wall, off to the side. If someone I know is with me, it's so much easier. Those triggers had controlled me before. I'm working on flipping that around and trying to control them now. I'm the one taking charge—not what's happening around me.

It's an entirely different world when I can be who I am and hang out with people who get me…when I hear the chatter in my head *and know exactly what it is. I always said there was nothing I could do about my anxiety. Wrong. I'm a human being and anxiety is a part of who I am. It's never going to completely go away but I'm not letting it define me. I know I'll likely need help for my entire life. I'll have setbacks and that's OK. It's what I choose to do about them that matters.*

INFORMATION AND RESOURCES

"Mental illness affects people of all ages, education, income levels, and cultures."

Canadian Mental Health Association

https://cmha.ca/fast-facts-about-mental-illness

The facts are staggering. The Canadian Mental Health Association states that…*in any given year, one in five people in Canada will personally experience a mental health problem or illness. By age forty, about fifty percent of the population will have or have had a mental illness.*

The impact on the lives of those affected cannot be overstated. Jackson's story is one example from millions of people around the world, who are struggling to figure out what is happening and what they can do to cope and survive every day. Though *Jackson* leaves us with hope and a promise of a healthy future after years of suffering, the reality is that not every young person has that outcome. Suicide accounts for twenty-four percent of all deaths among fifteen to twenty-four-year-olds in Canada (four times more likely for men). Twenty-four percent.

Almost one half (forty-nine percent) of those who feel they have suffered from depression or anxiety have never gone to see a doctor about this problem and only one in five children with mental-health problems receive mental health services.

Some of our barriers seem almost unsurmountable: People who don't accept they need help, believing they can deal with it on their own. Those who know they are not well but won't get support because of the perceived stigma attached. People who desperately want assistance but are put on wait lists or passed from one practitioner to another. Those who reside in communities where services are slim.

A bureaucratic system delivers and administers health-care services through provincial and territorial governments. We have primary, secondary, and supplementary services that are often fragmented and certainly not a "wrap around" model. It's so complex that private organizations are offering "health-care advocates" to help us navigate the system.

We have been far too slow to change in response to this growing crisis. But there is a movement that is gaining traction.

June and Craig are portrayals of typical parents who desperately find their way through each crisis, questioning themselves and carrying regrets. No one is prepared for what is thrown at them when a child can't find their way out of bed or doesn't believe there is a reason for being. But families need not struggle alone.

The Canadian Mental Health Association (https://cmha.ca/) has branches across the country. The ABCs of Mental Health is an exceptional resource website for parents and educators seeking to understand behaviours (https://www.sickkidscmh.ca/ABC/Welcome). Children's Mental Health Ontario (https://www.cmho.org/) has facts and youth and parent resources.

We have a National Suicide Helpline (1-800-273-8255), Kids Helpline (1-800-55-18000, Child and Youth Mental Health (https://ontario.cmha.ca/mental-health/child-and-youth-mental-health/), Community Crisis Centres, peer support groups, and many more services available today. The Canadian Alliance on Mental Illness and Mental Health (https://www.camimh.ca/), is a volunteer non-profit organization, which provides mental health education to the public. Regardless of where you live in the world, seek out the services available to you, whether they are driven by government programs or not-for-profit, reputable agencies.

Doctors, psychiatrists, counsellors, social workers, psychologists, and nurses are all professionals; registered or certified in mental health. June was desperate for her son to use a combination of medication and therapy, pushing Jackson in this direction because of her research. She knew he could be taught to recognize his triggers and learn how to change his responses to healthy ones.

What about the alternative options? In the past few years we have seen life and trauma coaches working with people. Others have turned to more "natural" remedies such as meditation, mindfulness training, yoga, nutritional supplements, CBD oil, or reiki. There are countless testimonials from those who have sought a solution outside of the medical world, found success, and now consider themselves mentally well. There is no "one" magic bullet. But without taking the first step, the person suffering will never know what intervention would make the difference.

In September of 2010, Bell Let's Talk was launched, with celebrities leading "the conversation" to end the stigma attached to mental health. Can we talk about depression openly and honestly? If we were diagnosed with a mental illness, could we discuss it with a friend in the same way we would if we had suffered a heart attack? What language do we use? Are we kind? Do we listen to understand? If we know someone is struggling, are we now stepping in to guide them towards the support they need? To date, Bell has raised over 100 million dollars, partnering with other organizations, creating community-fund grants, supporting research, and much more. This is one example of action that has resulted in significant change. https://letstalk.bell.ca/en/

What can we do as individuals? Plenty! I hope that this book empowers each of us to act in support of ourselves, a loved one, or anyone showing the symptoms of mental illness.

How do I know when to help? Some signs that a friend or family member may have a mental illness and could need your help are:
- *They suddenly no longer have interest in hobbies and other interests they used to love*
- *They seem to feel angry or sad for little or no reason*
- *They don't seem to enjoy anything anymore*
- *They have told you about or seem to be hearing strange voices or having*
- *unsettling thoughts*
- *They seem emotionally numb, like they don't feel anything anymore*
- *They used to be healthy, but now they're always saying they feel a bit sick*
- *They eat a lot more or less than they used to*
- *Their sleep patterns have changed.*
- *They seem to be anxious or terrified about situations or objects in life that*
- *seem normal to you and others.*
- *They've been missing more and more time from work or school.*
- *They've been drinking heavily and/or using drugs to cope.*
- *They are talking about taking their lives or feeling hopeless.*
- *They are avoiding their close friends and family members.*

https://www.heretohelp.bc.ca/infosheet/supporting-a-friend-or-family-member-with-a-mental-illness

We are much more aware than we have ever been in the past. Knowledge is power. We can't walk away, avoid contacting someone because we don't know what to say. Be there. Pick up the phone, drop in for a visit. It could be the moment you save someone's life.

ENDNOTES

1 **Mental Illness**

https://ww1.cpa-apc.org/MIAW/pamphlets/Youth.asp

Mental illness and mental disorder are not terms easy to define. Misunderstandings lead to misuse and abuse of the terminology, help reinforce myths, and even prevent people from getting help when it is really needed.

In general, mental illness refers to clinically significant patterns of behavioural or emotional functioning that are associated with some level or distress, suffering (pain, death), or impairment in one or more areas of functioning (e.g.; school, work, social and family interactions). At the basis of this impairment is a behavioural, psychological, or biological dysfunction, or a combination of these.

2 **Anxiety Disorder**

https://cmha.ca/documents/anxiety-disorders

Anxiety disorders are mental illnesses. The different types of anxiety disorders include:

Phobia: A phobia is an intense fear around a specific thing like an object, animal, or situation. Most of us are scared of something, but these feelings don't disrupt our lives. With phobias, people change the way they live in order to avoid the feared object or situation.

Panic Disorder: Panic disorder involves repeated and unexpected panic attacks. A panic attack is a feeling of sudden and intense fear that lasts for a short period of time. It causes a lot of physical feelings like a racing heart, shortness of breath, or nausea. Panic attacks can be a normal reaction to a stressful situation, or a part of other anxiety disorders. With panic disorder, panic attacks seem to happen for no reason. People who experience panic disorder fear more panic attacks and may worry that something bad will happen as a result of the panic attack. Some people change their routines to avoid triggering more panic attacks.

Agoraphobia: Agoraphobia is fear of being in a situation where a person can't escape or find help if they experience a panic attack or other feelings of anxiety. People with agoraphobia may avoid public places or even avoid leaving their homes.

Social-Anxiety Disorder: Social-anxiety disorder involves intense fear of being embarrassed or evaluated negatively by others. As a result, people avoid social situations. This is more than shyness. It can have a big impact on work or school performance and relationships.

Generalized Anxiety Disorder: Generalized anxiety disorder is excessive worry around a number of everyday problems for more than six months. This anxiety is often far greater than expected—for example, intense anxiety over a minor concern. Many people experience physical symptoms too,

₃ Depression

https://cmha.ca/documents/children-youth-and-depression

Depression is a type of mental illness called a mood disorder. Mood disorders affect the way you feel, which also affects the way you think and act. With depression, you may feel "down," hopeless, or find that you can't enjoy things you used to like. Many people who experience depression feel irritable or angry. And some people say that they feel "numb" all the time.

Recognizing depression in young people can be more difficult than recognizing depression in adults, because young people experience so many changes. You may wonder what is "normal" and what might be a problem. Also, many children and teens may not want to talk about their feelings, or may have their own explanations for their experiences. However, you may still notice the following changes.

Changes in feelings: Your child may show signs of being unhappy, worried, guilty, angry, fearful, helpless, hopeless, lonely, or rejected.

Changes in physical health: Your child may start to complain of headaches or general aches and pains that you can't explain. They may feel tired all the time or have problems eating or sleeping. Your child may unexpectedly gain or lose weight.

Changes in thinking: Your child may say things that indicate low self-esteem, self-dislike or self-blame—for example, they may only talk about themselves negatively. They may have a hard time concentrating. In some cases, they may show signs that they're thinking about suicide.

Changes in behaviour: Your child might withdraw from others, cry easily, or show less interest in sports, games, or other fun activities that they normally enjoy. They might over-react and have sudden outbursts of anger or tears over small incidents.

Some of these changes may be signs of mental health problems other than depression. It's important to look at the bigger picture: how intense the changes are, how they impact your child's life, and how long they last. It's particularly important to talk to your child if you've noticed several changes lasting more than two weeks.

4 **Borderline Personality Disorder**

https://www.camh.ca/en/health-info/mental-illness-and-addiction-index/borderline-personality-disorder

Borderline personality disorder (BPD) is a serious, long-lasting, and complex mental health problem. People with BPD have difficulty regulating or handling their emotions or controlling their impulses. They are highly sensitive to what is going on around them and can react with intense emotions to small changes in their environment. People with BPD have been described as living with constant emotional pain, and the symptoms of BPD are a result of their efforts to cope with this pain.

It is very common for someone with BPD to have other mental health problems. These include:

major or moderate to mild depression

substance use disorders

eating disorders

problem gambling

post-traumatic stress disorder (PTSD)

social phobia

bipolar disorder.

Sometimes it can be difficult to diagnose BPD because symptoms of a co-occurring disorder mimic or hide the symptoms of BPD. Relapse in one disorder may trigger a relapse in the other disorder.

5 **Life Coach** https://www.lifecoaching.com/pages/life_coaching.html

Life Coaching is a profession that is profoundly different from consulting, mentoring, advice, therapy, or counseling. The coaching process addresses specific personal projects, business successes, general conditions, and transitions in the client's personal life, relationships, or profession by examining what is going on right now, discovering what the obstacles or challenges might be, and choosing a course of action to make your life what you want it to be.

ARE YOU A BOOK CLUB MEMBER?

Book Clubs bring us together to discuss each other's opinions, likes and dislikes about a topic that matters to us. Each of us will have varying thoughts about Jackson and June's journeys because of our own personal experiences, knowledge, and beliefs. Enjoy these ten questions that could be explored in your reading club.

1. Did the characters seem believable to you? Did they remind you of anyone?
2. What aspects of the author's story could you most relate to?
3. What scene resonated with you most on a personal level? Why? How did it make you feel?
4. Were you satisfied or disappointed with the ending?
5. Do you have a new perspective after reading this book?
6. Were there any passages that stood out to you? Why?
7. If you could talk to the author, what burning question would you want to ask?
8. Were there times you disagreed with a character's actions? What would you have done differently?
9. What scene would you point out as the pivotal moment in the narrative? How did it make you feel?
10. As a parent, would you have shared the psychological assessment report with your child in similar circumstances?

Lynn McLaughlin is an award-winning author and host of the podcast, "Taking the Helm". Through her own experience, collaboration with other writers and hundreds of hours of research, Lynn has created "Time to Publish". She offers a program that is broken into four components which guides aspiring writers towards publishing their manuscript. A professional speaker and advocate, Lynn has spent her life devoted to ensuring each of us meets our full potential.

Lynn has recently retired as an educator after 31 years, serving in many roles including Superintendent of Education, Principal, Vice-Principal, French and Special Education teacher. Mother of three grown children, she currently lives with her husband in southern Ontario. She is an active Rotarian dedicated to community causes. Lynn is also a member of 100 Women Who Care Windsor/Essex and works tirelessly to support the goals of the Brain Tumour Foundation of Canada. She strives to meet each new personal goal and has just completed her first Detroit International ½ Marathon in November 2019.

Lynn is driven by a single mission: to lead and empower people to make conscious and positive choices. She writes with passion, sensitivity and insight, never losing sight of the reader. Her first book, "Steering Through It" and the experiences she shares, have become the catalyst for her work in advocacy today.

Every author hopes to receive reader reviews. It would be appreciated if you would kindly consider posting your review of "Jackson" for our reading community to enjoy.

Enjoy a free resource by going to Lynn's website and signing up for her mailing list. There is always something each month in "Lynn's Blitz" for you to enjoy as we learn from and with each other.

Enjoy this excerpt from the epilogue of another one of Lynn's books, Steering Through It.

"My tumour was meant to be. I clearly had lessons to learn in this life. I still do. I don't pretend to know what the future holds but do view things differently now. I consciously choose to make the best out of any given situation; not judge others but seek to understand; and find every opportunity to laugh, give support and love. We all have our trying moments, but if you've had to look in the mirror and wonder whether your life is coming to an end, you quickly realise that many things you once considered to be crises do not matter in the least. They are trivial in the grand scheme. Trust me. It's people that matter. Don't' wait for that moment when time stops. As yourself, "Am I living a happy, caring, fulfilling life that gives to others?" If we each could answer that question honestly, and be true to ourselves, can you imagine the possibilities?"

Lynn's Amazon Author Page

Printed in Canada